Mary Elizabeth Braddon

Strangers and Pilgrims

Vol. I

Mary Elizabeth Braddon

Strangers and Pilgrims
Vol. I

ISBN/EAN: 9783337050733

Printed in Europe, USA, Canada, Australia, Japan

Cover: Foto ©Andreas Hilbeck / pixelio.de

More available books at **www.hansebooks.com**

STRANGERS AND PILGRIMS

A Novel

BY THE AUTHOR OF

'LADY AUDLEY'S SECRET'

ETC. ETC. ETC.

> ' Egypt, thou knewst too well,
> My heart was to thy rudder tied by the strings,
> And thou shouldst tow me after ; o'er my spirit
> Thy full supremacy thou knewst ; and that
> Thy beck might from the bidding of the gods
> Command me.'

IN THREE VOLUMES

VOL. I.

LONDON

JOHN MAXWELL AND CO.

4 SHOE LANE, FLEET STREET

1873

STRANGERS AND PILGRIMS

CHAPTER I.

'Give me a look, give me a face,
That makes simplicity a grace;
Robes loosely flowing, hair as free:
Such sweet neglect more taketh me
Than all the adulteries of art;
They strike mine eyes, but not my heart.'

THE scene was an ancient orchard on the slope of a hill, in the far west of England : an orchard bounded on one side by an old-fashioned garden, where roses and carnations were blooming in their summer glory ; and on the other by a ponderous red-brick wall, heavily buttressed, and with a moat at its outer base—a wall that had been built for the protection of a more important habitation than Hawleigh Vicarage. Time was when the green slope where the rugged apple-

trees spread their crooked limbs in the sunshine was
a prim pleasance, and when the hill was crowned by
the grim towers of Hawleigh Castle.   But the civil
wars made an end of the gothic towers and machico-
lated galleries that had weathered many a storm, and
nothing was now left save a remnant of the old wall,
and one solitary tower, to which some archeologically-
minded vicar in time past had joined the modest
parsonage of Hawleigh parish.   This was a low
white building, of the farmhouse type, large and
roomy, with bow-windows to some of the lower rooms,
and diamond-paned casements to others.   In this
western land of warm rains and flowers the myrtles
and roses climbed to the steeply-sloping roof, and
every antique casement was set in a frame of foliage
and blossom.   It was not a mansion which a modern
architect would have been proud to have built, by any
means, but a dwelling-place with which a painter or
a poet would have fallen madly in love at first sight.

There were pigeons cooing and boop-boop-booping
among the moss-grown corbels of the tower; a black-
bird in a wicker cage hanging outside one of the narrow windows; a skylark in a little green wooden box
decorating another. The garden where the roses and
carnations flourished had somewhat of a neglected
look, not weedy or forlorn, only a little unkempt and

over-luxuriant, like a garden to which the hireling gardener comes once a week, or which is left to the charge of a single outdoor labourer, who has horses and pigs upon his mind, nay perhaps also the daily distraction of indoor duties, in the boot-and-knife-cleaning way.

Perhaps, looking at the subject from a purely poetical point of view, no garden should ever be better kept than that garden at Hawleigh. What ribbon-bordering, or artistically variegated mosaic of lobelia, and petunia, and calceolaria, and verbena, could ever equal the wild beauty of roses that grew at their own sweet will against a background of seringa and arbutus—shrubs that must have been planted by some unknown benefactor in the remote past, for no incumbent of late years had ever been known to plant anything? What prim platter-like circles of well-behaved bedding-out plants, spick and span from the greenhouse, could charm the sense like the various and yet familiar old-world flowers that filled the long wide borders in Parson Luttrell's flower-garden?

Of this small domain about half an acre consisted of meadow-like grass, not often improved by the roller, and sometimes permitted to flourish in rank luxuriance ankle-deep. The girls—that is to say, Wilmot Luttrell's four daughters—managed to play

croquet upon that greensward nevertheless, being at
the croquet-playing stage of existence, when a young
woman hard driven would play croquet in an empty
coal-cellar. Near the house the grass assumed form
and dignity, and was bordered by a rugged sweep of
loose gravel, called the carriage-drive; and just opposite the drawing-room windows there stood an
ancient stone sundial, on which the ladies of Hawleigh Castle had marked the slow passage of empty
hours in centuries gone by. Only a hedge of holly
divided the garden from a strip of waste land that bordered the dusty high-road; but a row of fine old elms
grew on that intervening strip of grass, and secured
the Luttrell damsels from the gaze of the vulgar.

But for seclusion, for the sweet sense of utter
solitude and retirement, the orchard was best—that
undulating slope of mossy turf, cropped close by occasional sheep, which skirted the flower-garden, and
stretched away to the rear of the low white house.
The very wall, crowned with gaudy dragon's-mouth,
and creeping yellow stonecrop, was in itself a picture;
and in the shelter of this wall, which turned its stalwart old back to the west, was the nicest spot for an
afternoon's idleness over a new book, or the worthless
scrap of lace or muslin which constituted the last
mania in the way of fancy-work. This, at least, was

what Elizabeth Luttrell said of the old wall, and as she had been born and reared for the nineteen years of her young life at Hawleigh, she was a tolerable judge of the capabilities of garden and orchard. She sits in the shadow of the wall this June afternoon alone, with an unread book in her lap.

Elizabeth Luttrell is the beauty of a family in which all the daughters are or have been handsome —the peerless flower among four fair sisters, who are renowned throughout this part of the western world as the pretty Miss Luttrells.

About Gertrude the eldest, or Diana the second, or Blanche the youngest, there might be differences of opinion—a question raised as to the length of Gertrude's nose, a doubt as to the width of Diana's mouth, a schism upon the merits of Blanche's figure; but the third daughter of the house of Luttrell was simply perfect: you could no more dispute her beauty than that of the Florentine Venus.

What a picture she made upon this midsummer afternoon, as she sat in the shade of the ruddy old wall, in a holland dress, and with a blue ribbon twisted in her hair, profile of face and figure in full relief against the warm background, every line the perfection of grace and beauty, every hue and every curve a study for a painter! O, if among all the splendid fashion-plates in the Royal Academy—the duchess in black-velvet train and point-lace flounces and scarlet-silk petticoat and diamonds; the marchioness in blue satin and blonde and pearls; the countess in white silk and azaleas; the viscountess in tulle and rose-buds—if in this feast of millinery Elizabeth Luttrell could but shine forth, sitting by the old orchard wall in her washed-out holland gown, what a revelation that fresh young beauty would seem!

It was not a rustic beauty, however—not a loveliness created to be dressed in white muslin and to adorn a cottage—but splendid rather, and worthy to rule the heart of a great man. Nose, a small aquiline; eyes, that darkly-clear gray which in some lights deepens to violet; complexion, a warm brunette; forehead, low and broad; hair of the darkest brown, with ruddy golden gleams lurking in its crisp waves —hair which is in itself almost a sufficient justification for any young woman to set up as a beauty, if her stock-in-trade were no more than those dark-brown tresses, those delicately-arched brows and up-ward curling lashes. In all the varying charms of expression, as well as in regularity of feature, Nature has gifted Elizabeth Luttrell with a lavish hand. She is the crystallisation of centuries of dead-and-gone Luttrells, all more or less beautiful; for the race is one that can boast of good looks as a family heritage.

She sits alone by the old wall, the western sunlight shining through the red and yellow flowers of the dragon's-mouth above her head; sits alone, with loosely-linked hands lying idle in her lap, and fixed dreaming eyes. It is nearly an hour since she has turned a leaf of her book, when a ringing soprano voice calling her name, and a shower of rose-leaves thrown across her face, scare away her day-dreams.

She looks up impatiently, angrily even, at Blanche, the hoyden of the family, who stands above her on the steep grassy slope, with a basket of dilapidated roses on her arm. The damsel, incorrigibly idle alike by nature and habit, has been seized with an industrious fit, and has been clipping and trimming the roses.

'What a lazy creature you are, Lizzie!' she exclaims. 'I thought you were going to put the ribbons on your muslin dress for this evening.'

'I wish you'd be good enough to concern yourself about your own clothes, Blanche, and leave mine alone. And please don't come screaming at me when I'm— asleep.'

'You weren't asleep; your eyes were ever so wide open. You were thinking—I can guess what about —and smiling at your own thoughts. I wish I had

anything as nice to think about. That's the worst
of having a handsome sister. How can I suppose
that any one will ever take any notice of poor little
me ?'

' Upon my honour, Blanche, I believe you are the
most provoking girl in creation !'

' You can't believe that, for you don't know all the
girls in creation.'

' One of the most, then ; but that comes of sending a girl to school. You have all the schoolgirl
vulgarities.'

' I'm sure I didn't want to go to Miss Derwent's,
Lizzie. It was Gertrude's fault, making such a fuss
about me, and setting papa at me. I'd much rather
have run wild at home.'

' I think you'd run wild anywhere, in a convent
even.'

' I daresay I should ; but that's not the question.
I want to know if you're going to wear your clean
white muslin, because my own toilet hinges on your
decision. It's a serious matter for girls who are allowed only one clean muslin a week.'

' I don't know ; perhaps I shall wear my blue,'
replies Elizabeth with a careless air, pretending to
read.

' You won't do anything of the kind. It's ever

so tumbled, and I know you like to look nice when
Mr. Forde is here. You're such a mean girl, Elizabeth Luttrell. You pretend not to care a straw how
you dress, and dawdle here making believe to read
that stupid old volume of travels to the Victoria
Thingembob, which the old fogies of the book-club
chose for us, instead of some jolly novel; and when
we've put on our veriest rags you'll scamper up the
back-stairs just at the last moment, and come down
a quarter of an hour after he has come, all over crisp
muslin flounces and fresh pink ribbons, just as if
you'd a French milliner at your beck and call.'

'I really can't help it, if I know how to put on
my things a little better than you and Diana. I'm
sure Gertrude is always nicely dressed.'

'Yes, Gertrude has the brand of Cain—Gertrude
is a born old maid; one can see it in her neck-ribbons
and top-knots. Now, how about the white muslin?'

'I wish you wouldn't worry, Blanche; I shall
wear exactly what I please. I will not be pestered
by a younger sister. What's the time?'

The fourth Miss Luttrell drags a little Geneva
silver watch from her belt by a black ribbon — a
silver watch presented to her by her father on her
fifteenth birthday—to be exchanged for a gold one

at some indefinite period of the Vicar's existence, when a gleam of prosperity shall brighten the dull level of his financial career. He has given similar watches to all his daughters on their fifteenth birthdays; but Lizzie's lies forgotten amongst disabled brooches and odd earrings in a trinket-box on her dressing-table. Elizabeth Luttrell does not care to note the progress of her days on a pale-faced Geneva timepiece, value something under five pounds.

'Half-past five by *me*,' says Blanche.

'Are you twenty minutes slow, or twenty minutes fast?'

'Well, I believe I'm five-and-twenty minutes slow.'

'Then I shall come to dress in half an hour. I wish you'd just tack those pink bows on my dress, Blanche—you're evidently at a loss for something to do.'

'Just tack,' repeats the younger sister with a wry face; 'you mean sew them on, I suppose. That's like people asking you to "touch" the bell, when you're comfortably coiled up in an easy-chair at the other end of the room. It sounds less than asking one to ring it; but one has to disturb oneself all the same. I don't see why you shouldn't sew on your own ribbons; and I'm dead-tired—I've been standing in the broiling sun for the last hour, trimming the roses, and trying to make the garden look a little decent.'

'O, very well; I can get my dress ready myself,' says Elizabeth with a grand air, not lifting her eyes from the volume in which she struggles vainly to follow the current of the Victoria Nyanza. Has not Malcolm Forde expressed a respectful wish that she were a little less vague in her notions of all that vast world which lies beyond the market-town and rustic suburbs of Hawleigh?

'Don't be offended, Lizzie; you know I always do anything you ask me. Where are the ribbons?'

'In the left-hand top drawer. Be sure you don't tumble my flounces.'

'I'll take care. I'm so glad you're going to wear your white; for now I can wear mine without Gertrude grumbling about my extravagance in beginning a clean muslin at the end of the week: as if people with any pretence to refinement ever made any difference in their gowns at the end of the week—as if anybody but utter barbarians would go grubby because it was Friday or Saturday! Mind you come up-stairs in time to dress, Lizzie.'

'I shall be ready, child. The people are not to be here till seven.'

'The people! As if you cared one straw about Jane Harrison or Laura Melvin and that preposterous brother of hers!'

'You manage to flirt with the preposterous brother, at any rate,' says Lizzie, still looking down at her book.

'O, one must get one's hand in somehow. And as if there were any choice of a subject in this God-forsaken place!'

'Blanche, how can you use such horrid expressions?'

'But it is God-forsaken. I heard Captain Fielding call it so the other day.'

'You are always picking up somebody's phrases. Do go and tack on those ribbons, or I shall have to do it myself.'

'And that would be a calamity,' cries Blanche, laughing, 'when there is anybody else whose services you can utilise!'

It was one of the golden rules of Elizabeth Luttrell's life that she should never do anything for herself which she could get any one else to do for her. What was the good of having three unmarried sisters —all plainer than oneself—unless one made some use of them? She herself had grown up like a flower, as beautiful and as useless; not to toil or spin—only to be admired and cherished as a type of God-given idle loveliness.

That her beauty was to be profitable to herself and to the world by and by in some large way, she regarded as an inevitable consequence of her existence. She had troubled herself very little about the future; had scarcely chafed against the narrow bounds of her daily life. That certainty of high fortune awaiting her in the coming years supported and sustained her. In the mean while she lived her life—a life not altogether devoid of delight, but into which the element of passion had not yet entered.

Even in so dull a place as Hawleigh there were plenty of admirers for such a girl as Elizabeth Luttrell. She had drunk freely of the nectar of praise; knew the full measure of her beauty, and felt that she was born to conquer. All the little victories, the trivial flirtations of the present, were, in her mind, mere child's play; but they served to give some variety to an existence which would have been intolerably monotonous without them.

She went on reading, or trying to read, for half an hour after Blanche had skipped up the green slope where the apple-trees spread a fantastic carpet of light and shade in the afternoon sunshine; she tried her hardest to chain her thoughts to that book of African travel, but the Victoria Nyanza eluded her like a will-o'-the-wisp. Her thoughts went back to a little scene under an avenue of ancient limes in Hawleigh-road—a scene that had been acted only a few hours ago. It was not very much to think of: only an accidental meeting with her father's curate, Malcolm Forde; only a little commonplace talk about the parish and the choir, the early services, and the latest volumes obtainable at the Hawleigh book-club.

Mr. Luttrell had employed four curates since Lizzie's sixteenth birthday; and the first, second, and third of these young Levites had been Lizzie's devoted slaves. It had become an established rule that the curate—Mr. Luttrell could only afford one, though there were two churches in his duty—should fall madly in love with Elizabeth. But the fourth curate was of a different stuff from the material out of which the three simpering young gentlemen fresh from college were created. Malcolm Forde was five-and-thirty years of age; a man who had been a soldier, and who had taken up this new service from conviction; a man who possessed an income amply sufficient for his own simple needs, and in no way looked to the Church as an honourable manner of solving the great enigma of how a gentleman is to maintain himself in this world. He was a Christian

in the purest and widest sense of the word ; an earnest thinker, an indefatigable worker ; an enthusiast
upon all subjects relating to his beloved Church.

To such a man as this all small flirtations and
girlish follies must needs appear trivial in the extreme ; but Mr. Forde was not a prig, nor was he
prone to parade his piety before the eyes of the world.
So he fell into the ways of Hawleigh with consummate
ease : played croquet with the mallet of a master ;
disliked high-jinks and grandiose entertainments at
rich people's houses, but was not above an impromptu
picnic with his intimate associates, a gipsy-tea in
Everton Wood, or a friendly musical evening at the
parsonage. He had little time to devote to such re-
laxations, but did not disdain them on occasion.

At the outset of their acquaintance the four Luttrell girls vowed they should always be afraid of him,
that those dreadful cold gray eyes of his made them
feel uncomfortable.

'When he looks at me in that grave searching
way, I positively feel myself the wickedest creature
in the world,' cried Diana, who was of a sprightly
disposition, and prone to a candid confession of all
her weaknesses. 'How I should hate to marry such
a man ! It would be like being perpetually brought
face to face with one's conscience.'

'I think a woman's husband ought, in a manner, to represent her conscience,' said Gertrude, who was nine-and-twenty, and prided herself upon being serious-minded. 'At least I should like to see all my faults and follies reflected in my husband's face, and to grow out of them by his influence.'

'What a hard time your husband would have of it, Gerty!' exclaimed the flippant Blanche, assisting at the conversation from outside the open window of the breakfast-room, or den, in which the four damsels were as untidy as they pleased; Elizabeth's colour-box and drawing-board, Gertrude's work-box, Diana's desk, Blanche's Dorcas bag, all heaped pell-mell upon the battered old sideboard.

'If you spent more time among the poor, Diana,' said Gertrude, not deigning to notice this interruption, 'you need not be afraid of any man's eyes. When our own hearts are at peace—'

'Don't, please, Gerty; don't give me any warmed-up versions of your tracts. The state of my own heart has nothing to do with the question. If I were the most spotless being in creation, I should feel just the same about Mr. Forde's eyes. As for district-visiting, you know very well that my health was never good enough for that kind of thing; and I'm sure if papa had six daughters instead of four, you do enough in the goody-goody line for the whole batch.'

Miss Luttrell gave a gentle sigh, and continued her needlework in silence. She could not help feeling that she was the one bit of leaven that leavened the whole lump; that if a general destruction were threatened the daughters of Hawleigh by reason of their frivolities, her own sterling merits might buy them off—as the ten righteous men who were *not* to be found in Sodom might have ransomed that guilty population.

Elizabeth had been busy painting a little bit of still-life—an over-ripe peach and a handful of pansies and mulberry-leaves lying loosely scattered at the base of Mr. Luttrell's Venetian claret-flask. She had gone steadily on with her work, laying on little dabs of transparent colour with a quick light touch, and not vouchsafing any expression of interest in the discussion of Mr. Forde's peculiarities.

'He's very good-looking,' Diana said meditatively. 'Don't you think so, Lizzie? You're an authority upon curates.'

Elizabeth shrugged her shoulders, and answered in her most indifferent tone:

'Tolerably! He has rather a good forehead.'

'Rather good!' exclaimed Gertrude, grinding in-

dustriously across an expanse of calico with her cutting - out scissors. 'He has the forehead of an
apostle.'

'How do you know that? You never saw an
apostle,' cried Blanche from the window, with her
favourite line of argument. 'And as for the pictures
we see of them, that's all humbug! for there were no
photographers in Judea.'

'Come indoors, Blanche, and write a German exercise,' said Gertrude. 'It's too bad to stand out
there all the morning, idling away your time.'

'And spoiling your complexion into the bargain,'
added Diana. 'What a tawny little wretch you are
becoming!'

'I don't care two straws about my complexion,
and I'm not going to cramp my hand with that
horrid German!'

'Think of the privilege of being able to read
Schiller in the original!' said Gertrude solemnly.

'I don't think much of it; for I never see you
read him, though you do pride yourself on your
German,' answered the flippant Blanche. And then
they went back to Mr. Forde, and discussed his eyes
and his forehead over again; not arriving at any
very definite expression of opinion at the last, and
Elizabeth holding her ideas in reserve.

'I don't think this one will be quite like the rest, Liz,' said Diana significantly.

'What do you mean by like the rest?'

'Why he won't make a fool of himself about you, as Mr. Horton did, with his flute-playing and stuff; and he won't go on like Mr. Dysart; and he won't write sentimental poetry, and languish about all the afternoon spooning at croquet, like little Mr. Adderley. You needn't count upon making a conquest of *him*, Lizzie. He has the ideas of a monk.'

'Abelard was destined to become a monk,' replied Elizabeth calmly, 'but that did not prevent his falling in love with Eloïse.'

'O, I daresay you think it will end by his being as weak as the rest. But he told me that he does not approve of a priest marrying — rather rude, wasn't it? when you consider that we should not be in existence, if papa had entertained the same opinion.'

'I don't suppose we count for much in his grand ideas of religion,' answered Elizabeth a little contemptuously. She had held her small flirtations with previous curates as the merest trifling, but the trifling had been pleasant enough in its way. She had liked the incense. And behold, here was a man who withheld all praise; who had made his own

scheme of life—a scheme from which she, Elizabeth
Luttrell, was excluded.   It was a new thing for her
to find that she counted for nothing in the existence
of any young man who knew her.

This conversation took place when Mr. Forde had
been at Hawleigh about a month.   Time slipped
past.   Malcolm Forde took the parish in hand with
a firm grip, Mr. Luttrell being an easy-going gentleman, quite agreeable to let his curate work as hard
as he liked.   The two sleepy old churches awoke
into new life.   Where there had been two services on
a Sunday there were now four; where there had been
one service on a great church festival there were now
five.   The dim old aisles bloomed with flowers at
Easter and Ascension, at Whitsuntide and Harvest-
thanksgiving-feast; and the damsels of Hawleigh
had new work to do in the decoration of the churches
and in the embroidery of chalice-covers and altar-
cloths.

But it was not in extra services and beautifica-
tion of the temples alone that Mr. Forde brought
about a new aspect of affairs in Hawleigh.   The poor
were cared for as they had never been cared for before.   Almost all the time that the soldier-curate
could spare from his public duties he devoted to
private ministration.   And yet when he did permit

himself an afternoon's recreation, he came to gipsy
tea-drinking or croquet with as fresh an air as if he
were a man who lived only for pleasure. Above all,
he never preached sermons—out of the pulpit. That
was his one merit, Lizzie Luttrell said, in a somewhat disparaging tone.

'His one fault is, to be so unlike the other curates, Liz, and able to resist your blandishments,'
said Diana sharply.

Mr. Forde had made himself a favourite with all
that household except Elizabeth. The three other
girls worshipped him. She rarely mentioned him
without a sneer. And yet she was thinking of him
this midsummer afternoon, as she sat by the orchard
wall, trying to read the volume he had recommended;
she was thinking of a few grave words in which he
had confessed his interest in her; thinking of the
dark searching eyes which had looked for one brief
moment into her own.

'I really thought I counted for nothing,' she said
to herself, 'he has such off-hand ways, and sets
himself so much above other people. I don't think he
quite means to be grand; it seems natural to him.
He ought to have been a general at least in India,
instead of a twopenny-halfpenny captain!'

The half-hour was soon gone. It was very plea-

sant to her, that idling in the shadow of the old
wall; for the thoughts of her morning's walk were
strangely sweet—sweeter than any flatteries that had
ever been whispered in her ear. And yet Mr. Forde
had not praised her; had indeed seemed utterly unconscious of her superiority to other women. His
words had been frank, and grave, and kindly : a little too much like a lecture, perhaps, and yet sweet ;
for they were the first words in which Malcolm Forde
had betrayed the faintest interest in her welfare.
And it is a hard thing for a young woman, who has
been a goddess and an angel in the sight of three
consecutive curates, to find the fourth as indifferent
to her merits as if he were a man of stone.

Yes, he had decidedly lectured her. That is to
say, he had spoken a little regretfully of her trivial
wasted life—her neglected opportunities.

' I don't know what you mean by opportunities,'
she had answered, with a little contemptuous curl of
the rosy upper lip. 'I can't burst out all at once
into a female bishop. As for district-visiting, I have
really no genius for that kind of thing, and feel myself a useless bore in poor people's houses. I know
I have been rather idle about the church embroidery,
too,' she added with a deprecating air, feeling that
here he had cause for complaint.

' I am very anxious that our churches should be made beautiful,' he answered gravely ; ' and I should think it only natural for you to take a delight in that kind of labour. But I do not consider ecclesiastical embroidery the beginning and end of life. I should like to see you more interested in the poor and in the schools, more interested in your fellow-creatures altogether, in short. I fancy the life you lead at Hawleigh Vicarage among your roses and apple-trees is just a little the life of the lotos-eater :

> " All its allotted length of days
>   The flower ripens in its place,
>   Ripens and fades and falls, and hath no toil,
>   Fast rooted in the fruitful soil."

It doesn't do for a responsible being to live that kind of life, you know, leaving no better memory behind than the record of its beauty. I should hardly venture to say so much as this, Miss Luttrell, if I were not warmly interested in you.'

The clear pale face, looking downward with rather a moody air, like the face of a wayward child that can hardly suffer a rebuke, flushed sudden crimson at his last words. To Mr. Forde's surprise ; for the interest he had confessed was of a purely priestly kind. But young women are so sensitive, and he was not

unused to see his female parishioners blush and
tremble a little under the magnetism of his earnest
gaze and low grave voice.

Conscious of that foolish blush, Elizabeth tried
to carry off her confusion by a rather flippant laugh.

'You read your Tennyson, you see,' she said,
'though you lecture me for my idleness. Isn't
poetry a kind of lotos-eating?'

'Hardly, I think. I don't consider my duty stern
enough to cut me off from all the flowers of life. I
should be sorry to moon about with a duodecimo
Tennyson in my pocket when I ought to be at work;
but when I have a stray half-hour, I can give myself
a little indulgence of that kind. Besides Tennyson
is something more than a poet. He is a teacher.'

'You will come to play croquet for an hour this
evening, won't you? Gertrude wrote to you yesterday, I think.'

'Yes, I must apologise for not answering her
note. I shall be most happy to come, if possible.
But I have two or three sick people to visit this afternoon, and I am not quite sure of my time. The
poor souls cling to one so at last. They want a
friendly hand to grasp on the threshold of the dark
valley, and they have some dim notion that we hold
the keys of the other world, and can open a door for

them and let them through to a better place than they could win for themselves.'

'It must be dreadful to see so much of death,' said Elizabeth, with a faint shudder.

'Hardly so dreadful as you may suppose. A deathbed develops some of the noblest qualities of a man's nature. I have seen so much unselfish thoughtfulness for others, so much tenderness and love in the dying. And then for these poor people life has been for the most part so barren, so troubled, it is like passing away from a perpetual struggle to a land that is to be all brightness and rest. If you would only spend more time among your father's parishioners, Miss Luttrell, you would learn much that is worth learning of life and death.'

'I couldn't endure it,' she answered, shrugging her shoulders impatiently; 'I ought never to have been born a parson's daughter. I should do no good, but harm more likely. The people would see how miserable I thought them, and be all the more discontented with their wretched lots after my visits. I can't act goody-goody as Gertrude does, and make those poor wretches believe that I think it the nicest thing in the world to live in one room, and have hardly bread to eat, and only one blanket among six. It's too dreadful. Six weeks of it would kill me.'

Mr. Forde sighed ever so faintly, but said no
more. What a poor, selfish, narrow soul this lovely
girl's must be! Nature does sometimes enshrine
her commonest spirits in these splendid temples.
He felt a little disappointed by the girl's selfishness
and coldness; for he had imagined that she needed
only to be awakened from the happy idleness of a
young joy-loving spirit. He said no more, though
they walked side by side as far as St. Mary's, the
red square-towered church at the beginning of the
town, and parted with perfect friendliness. Yet the
thought of that interview vexed Malcolm Forde all
day long.

'I had hoped better things of her,' he said to
himself. 'But of course I sha'n't give up. She is
so young, and seems to have a pliant disposition.
What a pity that Luttrell has let his daughters
grow up just as they please, like the foxgloves in
his hedges!'

In Mr. Forde's opinion, those four young women
ought to have been trained into a little band of sisters of mercy—a pious sisterhood carrying life and
light into the dark alleys of Hawleigh. It was not a
large place, that western market-town, numbering
eleven thousand souls in all; yet there were alleys
enough, and moral darkness and poverty and sickness

and sorrow enough, to make work for a nunnery of
ministering women. Mr. Forde had plenty of district-
visitors ready to labour for him; but they were for
the most part ill-advised and frivolous ministrants,
and absorbed more of his time by their need of counsel and supervision than he cared to give them. They
were of the weakest order of womanhood, craving
perpetual support and assistance, wanting all of them
to play the ivy to Mr. Forde's oak; and no oak, however vigorous, could have sustained such a weight of
ivy. He had to tell them sometimes, in plainest
words, that if they couldn't do their work without
continual recourse to him, their work was scarcely
worth having. Whereupon the weaker vessels dropped away, admitting in their High-Church slang that
they had no 'vocation;' that is to say, there was too
much bread and too little sack in the business, too
much of the poor and not enough of Mr. Forde.

For this reason he liked Gertrude Luttrell, who
went about her work in a workmanlike way, rarely
applied to him for counsel, had her own opinions, and
really did achieve some good. It may have been for
this reason, and in his desire to oblige Gertrude, that
he made a little effort, and contrived to play croquet
in the Vicarage garden on this midsummer evening.

CHAPTER II.

‘ Best leave or take the perfect creature,
   Take all she is or leave complete ;
 Transmute you will not form or feature,
   Change feet for wings or wings for feet.’

IT was halcyon weather for croquet; not a cloud in
the warm summer sky, and promise of a glorious
sunset, red and glowing, for ‘the shepherd's delight.’
The grass had been shorn that morning, and was
soft and thick, and sweet with a thymy perfume; a
little uneven here and there, but affording so much
the more opportunity for the players to prove themselves superior to small difficulties. The roses and
seringa were in their midsummer glory, and from the
white walls of the Vicarage came the sweet odours of
jasmine and honeysuckle, clematis and myrtle. All
sweet-scented flowers seemed to grow here with a
wilder luxuriance than Malcolm Forde had ever seen
anywhere else. His own small patrimony was on a
northern soil, and all his youthful recollections were
of a bleaker land than this.

'An enervating climate, I'm afraid,' he said to himself; and it seemed to him that the roses and seringa might be 'a snare.' There was something stifling in the slumberous summer air, the Arcadian luxury of syllabubs and cream, the verdure and blossom of this flowery land. He felt as if his soul must needs stagnate, as if life must become too much an affair of the senses, in so sweet and sensuous a clime.

This was but a passing fancy which flashed upon him as he opened the broad white gate and went into the garden, where the four girls in their white gowns and various ribbons were scattered on the grass: Blanche striking the last hoop into its place with her mallet; Diana trying a stroke at loose croquet; Gertrude busy at a tea-table placed in the shade of a splendid Spanish chestnut, which spread its branches low and wide, making a tent of greenery beneath which a dozen people could dine in comfort; Elizabeth apart from all the rest, standing by the sundial, tall, and straight as a dart, looking like a Greek princess in the days when the gods fell in love with the daughters of earthly kings.

Mr. Forde was not a Greek god, but a faint thrill stirred his senses at sight of that gracious figure by the sundial, nevertheless; only an artist's delight in

perfect beauty. The life which he had planned for
himself was in most things the life of a monk; but
he could not help feeling that Elizabeth Luttrell was
perfectly beautiful, and that for a man of a weaker
stamp there might be danger in this friendly association, which brought them together somehow two
or three times in every week.

'I have known her a year, and she has never
touched my heart in the faintest degree,' he told
himself, with some sense of triumph in the knowledge that he was impervious to such fascinations.
'If we were immortal, and could go on knowing each
other for thirty years—she for ever beautiful and
young, I for ever in the prime of manhood—I do
not think she would be any nearer to me than she is
now.'

Mr. Forde was the first of the guests. The three
girls ran forward to receive him, greeting him with a
kind of rapture. It was so good of him to come,
they gushed out simultaneously. They felt as if a
saint had come to take the first red ball and mallet.
Gertrude always gave Mr. Forde the red-ringed balls;
she said they reminded her of the rubric.

Elizabeth stirred not at all. She stood by the
sundial, her face to the west, comtemplative, or simply indifferent, Mr. Forde could not tell which. Did

she see him, he wondered, and deliberately refrain from greeting him? Or was she so lost in thought as to be unconscious of his presence? Or did she resent his little lecture of that morning? She could hardly do that, he considered, when they had parted in perfect friendship.

'It is so good of you to be punctual,' said Gertrude, making a pleasant little jingling with the china teacups; the best china, all blue-and-gold, hoarded away in the topmost of cupboards, wrapped in much silver paper, and only taken down for festive tea-drinkings like this.

It was not a kettledrum tea, but a rustic feast rather; or a 'tea-shuffle,' as young Mr. Melvin, the lawyer, called it. There was a round table, covered with a snowy table-cloth, and laden with home produce: a pound-cake of golden hue; preserved fruits of warm red and amber tint in sparkling cut-glass jars; that standing-dish on west-country tables, a junket; home-made bread, with the brown kissing crust that never comes from the hireling baker's oven; teacakes of feathery lightness; rich yellow butter, which to the epicure might have been worth a journey from London to Devonshire; and for the crowning glory of the banquet, a capacious basket of strawberries and a bowl of clotted cream.

'The Melvins are always late,' said Diana; 'but
we are not going to let you wait for your tea, Mr.
Forde—are we, Gertrude? Here comes Ann with the
kettle.'

This silver teakettle was the pride of the Luttrell
household. It had been presented to Mr. Luttrell at
the close of his ministrations in a former parish, and
was engraved with the Luttrell coat of arms in all
the splendour of its numerous quarterings. A spirit-
lamp burned beneath this sacred vessel, which Gertrude tended as carefully as if she had been a vestal
virgin watching the immortal flame.

Mr. Forde insisted that they should wait for the
rest of the company. He did not languish for that
cup of tea wherewith Miss Luttrell was eager to re-
fresh his tired frame. Perhaps in such a moment
his thoughts may have glanced back to the half-for-
gotten mess-table, and its less innocent banquets; the
long table, glittering in the low sunshine, with its
bright array of fairy glass and costly silver—was not
his corps renowned for its taste in these trifles?—
the pleasant familiar faces, the talk and laughter.
Time was when he had lived his life, and that altogether another life, differing in every detail from his
existence of to-day, holding not one hope, or dream,
or project which he cherished now. He could look

back at those idle pleasures, those aimless days,
without the faintest sigh of regret. Saddened, discouraged, fainthearted, he had often been since this
pilgrimage of his was begun; but never for one weak
moment had he looked longingly back.

He said a few words to Blanche, who blushed,
and sparkled, and answered him in little gasps, with
upward worshipping gaze, as if he had been indeed
an apostle; talked with Diana for five minutes or so
about the choir—she played the harmonium in St.
Mary's, the older of the two churches, which did not
boast an organ; and then strolled across the grass
to the sundial, where Lizzie was still standing in
mute contemplation of the western sky.

They shook hands almost silently. He did not
intend to apologise for what he had said that morning. If the reproof had stung her, so much the better. He had meant to reprove. And yet it pained
him a little to think that he had offended her. How
lovely she was as she stood before him, smiling, in
the western sunshine! He never remembered having
seen anything so beautiful, except a face of Guido's
—the face of the Virgin-mother—in a Roman picture-gallery. That smile relieved his mind a little.
She could hardly be offended.

'You have had a fatiguing day, I suppose, with

your sick people?' she said suddenly, after a few
words about the beauty of the evening and the un-
punctuality of their friends. 'Do you know, I have
been thinking of what you said to me this morning,
all day long; and I begin to feel that I must do something. It seems almost as if I had had what evan-
gelical people describe as "a call." I should really
like to do something. I don't suppose any good will
come of it—I know it is not my line—and I am rather
sorry you tried to awaken my slumbering conscience.
But you must tell me what I am to do. I am
your pupil, you know—your Madame de Chantal, St.
Francis!'

She looked up at him with her thrilling smile —
the deep violet eyes just lifted for a moment to his
own, with a glance which was swift and sudden as
the flight of an arrow. Across his mind there flashed
the memory of mediæval legends of witchcraft and
crime: records of priestly passion—of women whose
noxious presence had brought shame upon holy sis-
terhoods—of infatuation so fatal as to seem the inspiration of Satan—of baneful beauty that had lighted
the way to the torture-chamber and the stake. An
idle memory in such a moment! What had he to do
with those dark passions—the fungus-growth of an
age that was all darkness?

'I think your father is more than competent to advise you,' he answered gravely.

'O, no man is a prophet in his own country,' she said carelessly. 'I should never think of talking to papa about spiritual things; we have too many painful interviews upon the subject of pocket-money. If you want to reclaim me, you must help me a little, Mr. Forde. But, perhaps, I am not worth the trouble?'

'You cannot doubt that I should be glad to be of use to you. But it would be presumption on my part to dictate. Your own good sense will prompt you, and you have an admirable counsellor in your sister Gertrude, my best district-visitor.'

'I should never submit to be drilled by Gertrude. No; if you won't help me, I must wait for inspiration. As for district-visiting, I can't tell you how I hate the very notion of it. If there were another Crimean war now, I should like to go out as a nursing-sister, especially if'—she looked at him with another briefly mischievous glance—'if there were nice people to nurse.'

'I'm afraid, young ladies whose inclinations point to a military theatre are hardly in the right road,' he said coldly.

He felt that she was trifling with him, and was

inclined to be angry. He walked away from the sun-dial towards the hall-door, from which Mr. Luttrell was slowly emerging—an elderly gentleman; tall and stout, with a still handsome face framed in silky gray whiskers, and a slightly worn-out air, as of a man who had mistaken his vocation, and never quite re-covered his discovery of the mistake.

'Very good of you to come and play croquet with my children, Forde,' he said, in his good-natured lazy way—he had called them children when they were all in the nursery, and he called them children still—'especially as I don't think it's particularly in your line. O, here come the Melvins and Miss Harrison; so I suppose we are to begin tea, in or-der that you may have an hour's daylight for your game?'

Elizabeth had walked away from the sundial in an opposite direction, smiling softly to herself. It was something to have made him angry. She had seen the pale dark face flush hotly for a moment; a sudden fire kindled in the deep gray eyes. In the morning he had confessed himself interested in her welfare; in the evening she had contrived to provoke him. That was something gained.

'He is not quite a block of stone!' she thought.

She did not trouble herself to come forward and

welcome the Melvin party, any more than she had
troubled herself to greet Mr. Forde; but came strolling across the grass towards the tea-table presently when every one else was seated; the guests
here and there under the chestnut branches, while
Gertrude sat at the table dispensing the tea-cups,
with Frederick Melvin in attendance. Mr. Melvin
was the eldest son of the chief solicitor of Hawleigh,
in partnership with his father, and vaguely supposed
to be eligible from a matrimonial point of view. He
was a young man who had an unlimited capacity for
croquet, vingt-et-un, table-turning, and small flirtations; spent all his spare hours on the river Tabor,
and seemed hardly at home out of a suit of boating
flannels. He was indifferently in love with the four
Miss Luttrells, with a respectful leaning towards
Elizabeth, as the beauty; and he was generally absorbed by the flippant Blanche. His sister Laura
sang well, and did nothing else to particularise herself in the minds of her acquaintance. She was fond
of music, and discoursed learnedly of symphonies and
sonatas, adagios in C flat and capriccios in F double
sharp, to the terror of the uninitiated. Miss Harrison was a cousin, whose people were of the gentle-
man-farmer persuasion, and who came from a sleepy
old homestead up the country to stay with the Mel-

vins, and intoxicate her young senses with the dissi-
pations of Hawleigh market-place. The Melvins
lived in the market-place, in a big square brick house
picked out with white—a house with three rows of
windows five in a row, a flight of steps, and a green
door with a brass knocker; the very house, one would
suppose, upon which all the dolls' houses ever manu-
factured have been modelled. She was not a very
brilliant damsel; and when she had been asked how
she liked Hawleigh after the country, and how she
liked the country after Hawleigh, and whether she
liked Hawleigh or the country best, conversation with
her was apt to languish.

Mr. Forde, who was sitting a little in the background, talking to Mr. Luttrell, rose and gave his
chair to Elizabeth—the last comer. He brought another for himself and sat down again, and went on
with his talk; while Frederick Melvin worshipped at
Elizabeth's shrine—offering tea, and pound-cake, and
strawberries, and unutterable devotion.

'I wish you'd go and flirt with Blanche,' she said
coolly. 'No, thanks; I don't want any strawberries.
Now, please, don't sprinkle a shower of them on my
dress; I shall have to wear it a week. How awkward
you are!'

'Who could help being awkward?' pleaded the

youth, blushing. 'Sir Charles Grandison would have made a fool of himself in your society.'

'I don't know anything about Sir Charles Grandison, and I don't believe you do, either. That's the way with you young men; you get the names of people and things out of the *Saturday Review*, and pretend to know everything under the sun.'

'Wasn't he a fellow in some book—*Pamela*, or *Joseph Andrews?* something of Smollett's?—some sort of rubbish in sixteen volumes? Nobody reads it nowadays.'

'Then I wouldn't quote it, if I were you. But the *Saturday Review* is the modern substitute for the Eton Latin Grammar. Please, go and flirt with Blanche. You always stand so close to one, making a door-mat of one's dress!'

'O, very well; I'll go and talk to Blanche. But remember'—this with a threatening air—'when you want to go on the Tabor—'

'You'll take me, of course. I know that. Run and play, that's a dear child!'

He was her senior by three years, but she gave herself ineffable airs of superiority notwithstanding. Perhaps she was not displeased to exhibit even this trumpery swain before the eyes of Malcolm Forde— who went on talking of parish matters with her

father, as if unconscious of her presence. Very little
execution was done upon the pound-cake or the syllabub. The atmosphere was too heavily charged with
flirtation for any serious consumption of provisions.
It is the people who have done with the flowers and
sunshine of life who make most havoc among the
lobster-salads and raised pies at a picnic—for whom
the bouquet of the moselle is a question of supreme
importance, who know the difference between a hawk
and a heron in the way of claret.

So, after a little trifling with the dainty cates
Miss Luttrell had hospitably provided, the young
people rose for the business of the evening.

'Wouldn't you rather have a cigar and a glass of
claret here, under the chestnut?' said Mr. Luttrell,
as Malcolm Forde prepared to join them.

'That would be a breach of covenant,' answered
the Curate, laughing. 'I was invited for croquet.
Besides, I really enjoy the game; it's a sort of substitute for billiards.'

'A dissipation you have renounced,' said the
Vicar, in his careless way. 'You modern young men
are regular Trappists!'

Whereby it will be seen that Wilmot Luttrell was
of the Broad-Church party—a man who had hunted
the Devonian red-deer in his time, who had still a

brace of Joe Mantons in his study, was good at fly-
fishing, and did not object to clerical billiards or a
social rubber.

They played for a couple of hours in the balmy
summer evening, the Luttrell girls and their four
visitors—played till the sunlight faded into dusk,
and the dusk deepened into the soft June night—
which was hardly night, but rather a tender mixture of
twilight and starshine. Gertrude had taken Mr. Forde
for the leader of her side, Miss Harrison and Blanche
Luttrell making up their four. The Beauty headed a
skirmishing party, that incorrigible Frederick for her
supporter, Di Luttrell and Laura Melvin bringing up
the rear. To her Malcolm Forde addressed no word
throughout the little tournament. It may have been
because he had no opportunity; for she was laughing
and talking more or less all the time, in the wildest
spirits, with the young solicitor perpetually at her
elbow. And Gertrude had a great deal to say to the
Curate; chiefly on the subject of her parish work,
and a little of a more vague and metaphysical nature
concerning the impressions produced upon her mind
by his last Sunday-evening sermon. He listened
kindly and respectfully, as in duty bound, but that
frivolous talk and laughter upon the other side wor-
ried him not a little. Never had Elizabeth seemed

to him so vulgarly provincial; and he was really interested in her, as indeed it was his duty to be
interested in the welfare of his Vicar's daughters.

'It is all the father's fault,' he said to himself;
'I do not believe he has ever made the faintest attempt to train them.'

And then he thought what an estimable young
person Gertrude must be to have evolved out of her
inner consciousness, as it were, all that serious and
practical piety which made her so valuable to him in
his ministrations. As to the future careers of the
other three — of Blanche, who talked slang, and
seemed to consider this lower world designed to be
a perpetual theatre for flirtation; of Diana, who was
selfish and idle, and set up a pretence of weak health
as a means of escaping all the cares and perplexities
of existence; of Elizabeth, who appeared in her own
character to embody all the faults and weaknesses he
had ever supposed possible to a woman—of the manner in which these three were to tread the troubled
paths of life, he could only think with a shudder.
Poor lampless virgins, straying blindly into the darkness!

Yet, measured by a simply sensuous standard,
how sweet was that low rippling sound of girlish
laughter; how graceful the white-robed figure mov-

ing lightly in the summer dusk; how exquisite the dark-blue eyes that looked at him in the starlight, when the game was ended, and the Church Militant, as Blanche said pertly, had been triumphant over the Devil's Own, in the person of the mild-eyed Frederick Melvin! Mr. Forde's unerring stroke, mathematically correct as the pendulum, had brought them home, in spite of some rather feeble playing on the part of Gertrude, whose mind was a little too much occupied by last Sunday-evening's sermon.

Mr. Luttrell had strolled up and down the garden walk, smoking his cigar, and had loitered a little by the holly hedge talking to some people in the road, while the croquet players amused themselves. He came forward now to propose an adjournment to the house, and a claret-cup. So they all went crowding into a long low room with a couple of bow windows, a room which was lined with bookshelves on one side, containing Taylor and Hooker, and Barrow and Tillotson, and South and Venn, and other ecclesiastical volumes, freely intermingled with a miscellaneous collection of secular literature; a room which served Mr. Luttrell as a library, but which was nevertheless the drawing-room. There was a grand piano by one of the bow windows, a piano which had been presented to Diana by a wealthy aunt and godmother, and the brand-new walnut-wood case whereof was in strong contrast with the time-worn old chairs and tables; the cheffoniers of the early Georgian era; the ponderous old cane-seated sofa, with its chintz-covered pillows and painted frame—a pale, pale green picked out with gold that was fast vanishing away. The attenuated crystal girandoles upon the high wooden mantelshelf were almost as old as the invention of glass; the Chelsea shepherd and shepherdess had been cracked over and over again, but held together as if by a charmed existence. The Derbyshire-spa vases were relics of a dead-and-gone generation. The mock-venetian mirror was of an almost forgotten fashion and a quite extinct manufacture. Blanche vowed that Noah and his wife, when they kept house before the flood, must have had just such a drawing-room.

Yet this antiquated chamber seemed in no wise displeasing to the sight of Mr. Forde as he came in from the starlit garden. He liked it a great deal better than many finer rooms in which he was a rare but welcome visitor, just as he preferred the ill-kept Vicarage lawn and flower-borders to the geometrical parterres of millionaire cloth manufacturers or pompous squires on the outskirts of Hawleigh.

Frederick Melvin and his sister pleaded for a lit-

tle music, upon which the usual family concert began:
a showy fantasia by Gertrude, correctly played, with
a good firm finger, and not a spark of expression from
the first bar to the bang, bang, *bang!* at the end;
then a canzonet from Blanche, of the ' O, 'tis merry
when the cherry and the blossom and the berry, tra-
la-la-la, tra-la-la' school, in a thin little soprano;
then a sonata—Beethoven's ' Adieu'—by Miss Melvin, which Mr. Forde thought the longest adieu he
had ever been obliged to listen to. He lost patience
at last, and went over to Elizabeth, whose ripe round
mezzo-soprano tones he languished to hear.

' Won't you sing something?' he asked.

' What, does not singing come within your cata-
logue of forbidden pleasures—a mere idle waste of
time—lotos-eating, in short?'

' You know that I do not think anything of the
kind. Why do you try to make me out what I have
never pretended to be—an ascetic, or worse, a Phari-
see? Is it only because I am anxious you should be
of a little more use to your fellow-creatures?'

' And of course singing can be no use, unless I
went about among your cottage people leading off
hymns.'

' Does that mean that you won't sing to-night?'
he asked in his coldest tone.

' Yes.'

' Then I'll wish you good-night. I've no doubt the music we've been hearing is very good in its way, but it's hardly my way. Good-night. I'll slip away quietly without disturbing your friends.'

He was close to the open bow window, that farthest from the piano, and went out unnoticed, while Miss Melvin and her cousin Miss Harrison were debating whether they should or should not play the overture to *Zampa*. He went out of the window, and walked slowly across the grass, but had hardly reached the sundial, when he heard the voice he knew so well swell out rich and full in the opening tones of a ballad he loved, a plaintive lament called ' Ettrick.'

' O, murmuring waters, have you no message for me?"

He stopped by the sundial and heard the song to the end ; heard Fred Melvin supplicating for another song, and Elizabeth's impatient refusal—' She was tired to death,' with a little nervous laugh.

He went away after this, not offended, only wondering that any woman could be so wilful, could take so much pains to render herself unwomanly and unlovable. He thought how keenly another man, whose life was differently planned, might have felt this petty slight—how dangerous to such a man's peace Eliza-

beth Luttrell might have been; but that was all.
He was not angry with her.

What would he have thought, if he could have
seen Elizabeth Luttrell half an hour later that night,
if he could have seen her fall on her knees by one of
the little French beds in the room that she and
Blanche occupied together, and bury her face in the
counterpane and burst into a passion of tears?

'What is the matter, Liz—what is it, darling?'
cries Blanche the impulsive.

The girl answers nothing, but sobs out her brief
passion, and then rises, calm as a statue, to confront
her sister.

'If you are going to worry me, Blanche, I shall
sleep in the passage,' she exclaims in impatient rebuke of the other's sympathetic caress. 'There's
nothing the matter. I'm tired, that's all, and that
absurd Fred of yours has persecuted me so all the
evening.'

'He's no Fred of mine, and I think you rather
encouraged his persecutions,' said Blanche with an
aggrieved air. 'I'm sure I can't make you out, Lizzie.
I thought you liked Mr. Forde, and yet you quite
snubbed him to-night.'

'Snubbed him!' cried Elizabeth. 'As if anybody
could snub St. Paul!'

CHAPTER III.

THE Curate of Hawleigh, modest in his surroundings
as the incorruptible Maximilian Robespierre himself,
had lodgings at a carpenter's. His landlord was certainly the chief carpenter of the town, a man of un-
blemished respectability, who had even infused a
flavour of building into his trade ; but the Curate's
bedroom windows commanded a view of the carpenter's
yard, and he lived in the odour of chips and shavings,
and that fresh piney smell which seems to breathe
the perfume of a thousand ships far away upon the
barren main. He had even to submit meekly to the
dismal tap, tap, tap of the hammer when a coffin was
on hand, which might fairly serve as a substitute for
the ' *Frère, il faut mourir!*' of the Trappist brotherhood.

It must not be supposed, however, that this choice

of a lodging was an act of asceticism or wanton self-humiliation upon the part of Malcolm Forde. The Hawleigh curates lodged, as a rule, with Humphreys the carpenter; and Hawleigh being self-governed, for the most part, upon strictly conservative principles, it would have been an outrage against the sacred existing order of things if Mr. Forde had pitched his tent elsewhither. Mrs. Humphreys was a buxom middle-aged woman of spotless cleanliness, who kept a cow in a neat little paddock behind the carpenter's yard; a woman who had a pleasant odour of dairy about her, and who was supposed by long practice to have acquired a special faculty for 'doing for curates.'

'I knows their tastes,' she would say to her gossips, 'and it's astonishing how little their tastes varies. "O, give me a chop, Mrs. Humphreys," they mostly says, if I werrit them about their dinner. But, lor, I know better than that. Their poor stomachs would soon turn against chops if they had them every day. So I soon leaves off asking 'em anything about dinner, and contrives to give 'em a nice variety of tasty little dishes—a whiting and a lamb cutlet or two with fried parsley one day; a red mullet and a split fowl broiled with half-a-dozen mushrooms the next, a spitchcook, *they* call it; and then the day

after I curry what's left of the fowl, so as their bills
come moderate ; and I never had a wry word with any
curate yet, except Mr. Adderley, who didn't like
squab-pie, and I did give him a piece of my mind
about *that*.'

The rooms were comfortable rooms, though of the
plainest ; lightsome and airy ; furnished with chairs
and tables so substantial that their legs had not been
enfeebled by the various fidgetinesses of a whole
generation of curates : honest wide-seated leather-
bottomed chairs bought at the sack of an ancient
manor-house ; stalwart walnut-wood tables and brass-
handled chests of drawers made when George the
Second was king. Mrs. Humphreys was wont to
boast that her Joe—meaning Mr. Joseph Humphreys
—knew what chairs and tables were, and did not
choose them for their looks. There were no ornaments of the usual lodging-house type, for Mrs. Humphreys knew that it is in the nature of curates to bring
with them sundry nicknacks, the relics of university
extravagances, wherewith to decorate their chambers.

Mr. Forde had furnished both sitting-room and
bedroom amply with books, nay even the slip of a
chamber where he kept his baths and sponges and
bootstand was encumbered with the shabbier volumes
in his collection, piled breast-high in the angles of

the walls. He was not a collector of bric-à-brac, and the sole ornaments of his sitting-room were a brass skeleton clock which had travelled many a league with him in his soldiering days; a carefully painted miniature of an elderly lady, whom, by the likeness to himself, one might reasonably suppose to be his mother, on one side of the mantelpiece; a somewhat faded daguerreotype of a sweet fair young face on the other; and a breakfast cup and saucer on a little ebony stand under a glass shade. Why this cup and saucer should be so preserved would have been a puzzling question for a stranger. They were of ordinary modern china, and could have possessed no value from an artistic point of view.

He had performed his early morning duty at St. Clement's, and spent half an hour with a sick parishioner, before his nine-o'clock breakfast on the day following that little croquet party at the Vicarage. He was dawdling a little as he sipped his second cup of tea, with one of Southey's Commonplace Books open at his elbow, turning over the leaves now and then with a somewhat absent air, as if in all that jetsam and flotsam of the poet's studious hours he hardly found a paragraph to enchain his attention.

What manner of man is he, in outward semblance, as he sits there absent and meditative, with the broad

summer daylight on his face ? It would be a question
if one should call him a handsome man.   He is dis-
tinguished-looking, perhaps, rather than handsome ;
tall and broad-shouldered, like the men who come
from beyond the Tweed; straight as a dart; a man
who is not dependent upon dress and surroundings
for his dignity, but has an indefinable air of being
superior to the common herd. His features are good,
but not particularly regular, hardly coming within
the rule and compass of archetypal beauty ; the nose
a thought too broad, the forehead too dominant. His
skin is dark, and has little colour, save when he is
angry or deeply moved, when the stern face glows
briefly with a dark crimson. The clear cold gray eyes
are wonderful in their variety of expression.   The
firmly-moulded yet flexible mouth is the best feature
in his face, supremely grave in repose, infinitely
tender when he smiles.

He smiles suddenly now, in the course of his
reverie, for it is clear enough that he is thinking, and
not reading Southey's agreeable jottings, though his
hand mechanically turns the leaves. He smiles a slow
thoughtful smile.

'What a child she is,' he says to himself, 'with
all a child's perversity ! I am foolish ever to be angry
with her.'

He heard a double-knock from the little brass knocker of Mr. Humphreys' private door, shut his book with an impatient sigh, got up, and walked to the window. The Humphreys mansion was in one of the side streets of Hawleigh, a street known by the rustic title of Field-lane, which led up a gentle hill to the open country; a vast stretch of common-land, sprinkled sparsely on the outskirts with a few scattered houses and a row or two of cottages. Nor had Mr. Humphreys any opposite neighbours; the houses on the other side stopped abruptly a few yards below, and there was a triangular green, with a pond and a colony of ducks in front of the Curate's casements.

Malcolm Forde looked out of the window, expecting to see his visitor waiting meekly on the spotless doorstep; but the door had been opened promptly, and the doorstep was unoccupied. He looked at his watch hastily.

'I've been wasting too much time already,' he said to himself, 'and here is some one to detain me ever so long. And I want to make a good morning's round out Filbury way.'

The medical practitioners of Hawleigh prided themselves on the crushing nature of their duties, yet there was none among them who worked so hard

as this healer of souls. Here was some tiresome
vestryman, perhaps, come to prose for half an hour
or so about some pet grievance, while he was languishing to be up and doing among the miserable hovels
at Filbury, where, amidst the fertile smiling land-
scape, men's souls and bodies were consuming away
with a moral dry-rot.

The door of his sitting-room opened, but not to
admit a prosing vestryman. The smiling handmaiden
announced 'Miss Luttrell, if you please, sir.' And,
lo, there stood before him on the threshold of his
chamber the wilful woman he had been thinking
about just now, gravely regarding him, the very image
of decorum.

There was some change in her outward aspect,
the details whereof his masculine eye could not dis-
tinguish. A woman could have told him in a moment by what means the Beauty had contrived to
transform herself. She was dressed in a lavender-
cotton gown, with tight plain sleeves, and a linen
collar—no bright-hued ribbon encircling the long
white throat, no flutter of lace or glimmer of golden
locket, none of the pretty frivolities with which she
was accustomed to set-off her loveliness. She wore
an old-fashioned black-silk scarf, a relic of her dead
mother's wardrobe, which became her tall slim figure

to perfection. She, who was wont to wear the most coquettish and capricious of hats, the daintiest conceit in airy tulle by way of a bonnet, was now crowned with a modest saucer-shaped thing of Dunstable straw, which at this moment hid her eyes altogether from Malcolm Forde. The rich brown hair, which she had been accustomed to display in an elaborate structure of large loose plaits, was neatly braided under this Puritan headgear, and packed into the smallest possible compass at the back of her head. She had a little basket in one hand, a red-covered account-book in the other.

'If you please, Mr. Forde, I should like you to give me a round of visits amongst your poor people,' she said, offering him this little volume. 'I am quite ready to begin my duties to-day.'

He stood for a moment gazing at her, lost in amazement. The provoking saucer-shaped hat covered her eyes. He could only guess the expression of her face from her mouth, which was gravity itself.

'What, Miss Luttrell, do you mean to help me, after all you said last night?'

'Did I really say anything very wicked last night?' she asked naïvely, lifting her head for a moment so that her eyes shone out at him under the shadow of the saucer brim. Peerless eyes they seemed to him in that brief flash, but hardly the most appropriate eyes for a district-visitor, whose beauty should be of a subdued order, like the colours of her dress.

'I don't know that you said anything wicked; but you expressed a profound disgust for district-visiting.'

'Did I? It was the last rebellious murmur of my unregenerate heart. But you have awakened my conscience, and I mean to turn over a new leaf, to begin a new existence in fact. If the piano were my property, instead of Diana's, I think I should make a bonfire on the lawn and burn it. I have serious thoughts of burning my colour-box—Winsor and Newton's too, and papa's last birthday present. But you must be kind enough to make me out a list of the people you'd like me to visit. I don't want to be a regular district-visitor, or to interfere with your established sisterhood in any way; so I won't take any tickets to distribute. I don't want the people to associate me with sacramental alms. I want to have a little flock of my own, and to see if I can make them like me for my own sake, without thinking how much they can get out of me. And if you could coach me a little about what I ought to say to them, it would be a great comfort to me. Gertrude says that when she feels herself at a loss she says a little prayer, and waits on the doorstep for a few minutes, till something comes to her. But I'm afraid that plan would not answer for me.'

Mr. Forde pushed one of the heavy chairs to the writing-table near the window, and asked Miss Luttrell to sit down while he wrote what she wanted in the little red book. She seated herself near one end of the table, and he sat down to write at the other.

'I shall be very happy to do what I can to set you going,' he said, as he wrote; 'but I should be more assured of your sincerity if you were less disposed to make a joke of the business.'

'A joke!' exclaimed Miss Luttrell with an aggrieved air; 'why, I was never in my life so serious. Is this the way in which you mean to treat my awakening, Mr. Forde?'

He handed her the little book, with a list of names written on the first leaf. 'I think you must know something of these people,' he said, 'after having lived here all your life.'

'Please don't take anything for granted about me with reference to the poor,' she answered hastily. 'Of course it is abominable in me to admit as much, but I never have cared for them. The only ideas

about them that I have ever been able to grasp are,
that they never open their windows, and that they
always want something of one, and take it ill if one
can't give them the thing they want. Gertrude tells
quite a different story, and declares that the serious-
minded souls are always languishing for spiritual refreshment, that she can make them quite happy with
her prim little sermons and flimsy little tracts. Did
you ever read a tract, Mr. Forde ? I don't mean a
controversial pamphlet, or anything of that kind ;
but just one of those little puritanical booklets that
drop from Gertrude like leaves from a tree in autumn ?'

'I have not given much leisure to that kind of
study,' replied Malcolm, with his grave smile. 'I
hope you won't think me unappreciative of the honour involved in this visit, Miss Luttrell, if I am
obliged to run away. I have a round of calls at Filbury to get through this morning.'

'You remind me of poor mamma,' said Elizabeth,
with a tributary sigh to the memory of that departed
parent ; 'she had always a round of calls, and they
generally resolved themselves into three—a triangle
of calls, in short. But they were genteel visits, you
know. Mamma never went in for the district business.'

The loose slangy style of her talk grated upon his
ear not a little.   He took his hat and gloves from the
sideboard—a gentle reminder that he was in haste to
be gone.

'I won't detain you five minutes more,' she said.
'How nice the room looks with all those books!   I
know Mrs. Humphreys' drawing-room very well,
though this is my first visit to you.   Papa and Gertrude and I came once to drink tea with Mr. Horton.
He gave quite a party; and we had concertante duets
for the flute and piano—"Non piu mesta," and "Di
piacer," and so on,' this with a faint blush, remembering her own share in that concerted music.   'You
should have seen the room in his tenancy—Bohemian-
glass vases, and scent caskets, and stereoscopes, and
photograph albums; but very few books.   I think I
like it best with all those grim-looking brown-backed
volumes of yours.'

She made the tour of the room as she spoke, and
paused by the mantelpiece to examine the skeleton
clock, the cup and saucer, the two portraits.

'What a grand-looking old lady!—your mother,
of course, Mr. Forde?   And, O, what a sweet face!'
pausing before the photograph.   'Your sister, I suppose?'

'No,' Mr. Forde answered, somewhat shortly.

'And what a pretty cup and saucer, under a glass shade! It looks like a relic of some kind.'

'It is a relic.'

The tone was grave, repellent even, and Elizabeth felt she had touched upon a forbidden subject.

'It belonged to his mother, I daresay,' she thought; 'and he keeps it in memory of the dead. I suppose all his people are dead, as he never talks about them.'

After this she made haste to depart with her little book, knowing very well that she had outraged all the conventionalities of Hawleigh, but rather proud of having bearded this lion of Judah in his den.

Mr. Forde left the house with her, and walked a little way by her side; but was graver and more silent than his wont, as if he had hardly recovered from the pain those injudicious questions of hers had given him. He parted from her at the entrance to a row of cottages, in which dwelt two of the matrons whose names he had entered in her book.

'Good-bye,' he said. 'I hope you will be able to do some good, and that you will not be tired of the work in a week or two.'

'That's rather a depressing suggestion,' said Elizabeth. 'I know you have the worst possible opinion of me; but I mean to show you how mistaken you have been. And you really ought to feel flattered by my conversion. Papa might have preached at me for a twelvemonth without producing such an effect.'

'I am sorry to hear that your father has so little influence with you, Miss Luttrell,' the Curate answered gravely.

He left her with the coldest good-bye. The proud face flushed crimson under the mushroom-hat as she turned into the little alley. This morning's interview had not been nearly so agreeable to her as yesterday's lecture under the limes at the entrance to the town. She began her missionary work in a very bad humour; but brightened by degrees as she went on. She was a woman in whom the desire to please dominated almost every other attribute, and she was bent upon making these people like or even love her. It was not to be a mere spurt, this adoption of a new duty. She meant to show Malcolm Forde that she could be all, or more than all, he thought a woman should be—that she could be as much Gertrude's superior in this particular line as she surpassed her in personal beauty.

'Gertrude!' she said to herself contemptuously. 'As if poor people could possibly care about Gertrude, with her little fidgety ways, and her Low-Church

tracts, and her passion for soapsuds and hearthstone!
She has contrived to train her people into a subdued
kind of civility. They look upon her visits as a
necessary evil, and put up with them, just as they
put up with the water coming through the roof, or a
pigsty close to the parlour window. But I shall make
my people look forward to my visits as a bright little
spot in their lives.'

This was rather an arrogant idea, perhaps; but
Elizabeth Luttrell succeeded in realising it. She
contrived to win an unfailing welcome in the twenty
cottages which Mr. Forde had assigned to her. Nor
was her popularity won by bribery and corruption.
She had very little to give her people, except an occasional packet of barley-sugar or a paper of biscuits
for the children, or now and then some cast-off ribbon
or other scrap of genteel finery for the mothers. For
the sick children, indeed, she would do anything—
empty her own slenderly furnished purse, rob the
cross old parsonage cook of her arrowroot, and loaf-
sugar, and isinglass, and cornflour, and ground rice,
and Epps's cocoa, and new-laid eggs; but it was not
by gifts of any kind that she made herself beloved.
It was the brightness and easy grace of her manner
rather, that delightful air of being perfectly at home
in a tiny chamber with a reeking washtub at her

elbow, a cradle at her knee, and a line of damp clothes steaming in close proximity to her hat. Nothing disgusted her. She never wondered that people could live in such dirt and muddle. She made her little suggestions of improvement—not blunt plain-spoken recommendation of soapsuds and hearthstone, but insinuating hints of what might be done with a little trouble—in a manner that never offended. And then she was so beautiful to look upon ; the husbands and wives were never tired of admiring her. 'Ay, but she be a rale right-down beauty,' they said, 'and thinks no more of herself than if she was as ugly as sin ;' not knowing that the fair Elizabeth was quite conscious of her own loveliness, and hoped to turn it to some good account by and by.

Nor did Elizabeth forget, in her desire for popularity, that the chief object of her mission among these people was of a spiritual kind ; that she was to carry enlightenment and religion into those close pent-up hovels where the damp linen was for ever dangling, the washtub for ever reeking ; where the larder was so often barren, and the wants of mankind so small and yet sometimes perforce unsatisfied. Although she was not herself, as Gertrude expressed it, 'seriously minded,' though her thoughts during her father's sermons, and even during those of Mr. Forde, too often wandered among the bonnets and mantles of the congregation, or shaped themselves into vague visions of the future, she did notwithstanding contrive to bring about some improvement in the theory and practice of her clients. She persuaded the women to go to church on Sunday evenings, if Sunday-morning worship was really an impossible thing, as the poor souls protested; she induced the husbands to clean themselves a couple of hours earlier than had been their Sabbath custom, and to shamble into the dusky aisle of St. Clement's or St. Mary's, while the tinkling five-minutes bell was still calling to loiterers and laggards on the way; she taught the little ones their catechism, rewarding proficiency with barley-sugar or gingerbread; and she sat by many a wash-tub reading the Evangelists in her full sweet voice, while the industrious housewife rubbed the sweats of labour from her husband's shirt-collars. She would even starch and iron a handful of collars herself, on occasion, if the housewife seemed to set about the business clumsily.

'I have to get-up my own fine things sometimes, or I should go cuffless and collarless,' she said. 'Papa is not rich, you know, Mrs. Jones.' Whereat Mrs. Jones would be struck with amazement by her handiness.

'I don't believe there's a thing in this 'varsal world as you can't do, Miss Elizabeth,' the admiring matron would cry with uplifted hands; and even this humble appreciation of her merits pleased Lizzie Luttrell.

Her reading was much liked by listeners who were not compelled to sit with folded hands and a brain perplexed by the thought of neglected housework. She had a knack of choosing the most attractive as well as the most profitable portions of Holy Writ, an acute perception of the passages most likely to impress her hearers.

'I do like *your* Scriptures, Miss Elizabeth,' said one woman. 'When I was a gal, I used to think the Bible was all Saul and the Philistings—there seemed no end of 'em—and David. I make no doubt David was a dear good man, and after the Lord's own heart; but there did seem too much of him. He wasn't like Him as you read about; he didn't come home to us like that, miss, and you don't read as *he* was fond of little children, except that one of his own that he was so wrapt up in.'

'The Gospel sounds like a pretty story, when you read it, miss,' said another; 'and when Miss Gertrude read, it did seem so sing-song like. Sometimes I couldn't feel as there was any sense in it, no more than in the Lessons of a hot summer's afternoon, when it seems only a droning, like a hive of bees.'

So Elizabeth went on and prospered, and grew really interested in her work. It was not half so bad as she had supposed. There was muddle and there was want, but not such utter gloom and misery as she had imagined in these hovels. The spirits of these people were singularly elastic. Ever so little sunshine warmed them into new life; and, above all, they liked her, and praised her, and spoke well of her to Malcolm Forde. She knew that from his approving manner, not from anything he had distinctly said upon the subject.

Rarely had she met with him on her rounds. The list he had given her included only easy subjects —people who would not be likely to repulse her attentions, homes in which she would not hear foul language or see dreadful sights—and having allotted her path-way, he was content that she should follow it with very little assistance from him, and even took pains to time his own visits, so as to avoid any encounter with her.

He did, however, on rare occasions find her among his flock. Not easily did he forget one summer afternoon, when he saw her sitting by an open cottage window with a sick child in her lap. That figure in a pale muslin dress, with the afternoon sunshine upon it, lived in his memory long.

'If I could only believe that she was quite in earnest,' he said to himself, 'that this new work of hers has some safer charm than its novelty, I should think her the sweetest woman I ever met—except one.'

Elizabeth had been engaged in these duties for two months, and had done her work faithfully. It was the end of August, the brilliant close of a summer that had been exceptionally fine; harvest just begun in this western land, and occasional tracts of tawny stubble baking under a cloudless blue sky; hazel-nuts and wortle-berries ripening in the woods; great sloe-trees shedding their purple fruit in every hedge; a rain of green apples falling on the orchard grass with every warm south wind; the red plums swelling and purpling on the garden wall—a vision of plenty and the perfume of roses and carnations on every side.

'If we don't have that picnic you talked about very soon, Gerty, we sha'n't have it at all,' remarked the youngest and the pertest of the four sisters at breakfast one morning, when Mr. Luttrell had withdrawn himself to his daily duties, and the damsels were left to enjoy half an hour's idleness and talk over empty coffee-cups and shattered eggshells and other fragments of the feast. 'The summer's nearly over, you see, Gerty, and if we don't take care we shall lose all the fine weather. I've no doubt there'll be a deluge after all this sunshine.'

Blanche always called her eldest sister 'Gerty' when she wanted some indulgence from that important personage.

'Well, I'm sure I don't know what to say, Blanche,' replied Miss Luttrell with provoking coolness, as if picnics and all such sublunary pleasures were utterly beneath her regard; strong, too, in her authority as her father's housekeeper, and conscious that her sisters must bow down and pay her homage for whatever they wanted, like Joseph's brethren in quest of corn. 'I really think,' she went on with a deliberate air, 'as the summer is nearly gone, we may as well give up any notion of a picnic this year, especially as papa doesn't seem to care about it.'

'Papa never seems to care about anything that costs money,' cried the disrespectful youngest. 'He'd like life well enough if everything in it could be carried on for nothing; if his children could be born and educated, and fed and clothed, and doctored and nursed, and introduced to society gratis, so that he could have all the pew-rents and burial-fees and things to put in the bank. It's very mean of you to talk like that, Gertrude, and want to sneak out of the picnic, when it's about the only return we're likely to make for all the croquet parties and dinners and teas and goodness knows what that our friends have given us since Christmas.'

'Really, Blanche, you are learning to render yourself eminently disagreeable,' Miss Luttrell observed severely, 'and I fear if papa does not face the necessity of sending you back to school to be finished, your deficiency in manner will be your absolute ruin in after-life.'

'Never mind Blanche's manner,' interposed Diana, 'but let's talk about the picnic. Of course we must have one. We always have had one for the last five years, since the summer after poor mamma's death,— I know we were all in slight mourning at the first of them,—and our friends expect it. So the only question is, where are we to go this year?'

This was intended in somewise as an assertion of independence on the part of the second Miss Luttrell, who did not intend to be altogether overridden by the chariot of an elder sister, even though that elder had bidden a long farewell to the golden summertide of her twenty-eighth year.

'Elizabeth won't go, of course, now she's turned serious,' said Blanche, with a sly glance at Lizzie, who sat leisurely watching the skirmish, with her head against the clumsy frame of the lattice, and the south wind gently stirring her dark-brown hair, a perfect picture of idle loveliness.

'You'll have nothing to do with the picnic, of course, Lizzie, not even if Malcolm Forde goes,' pursued the 'Pickle' of the family.

'Who gave you leave to call him Malcolm?' flashed out Elizabeth.

'No one; but why shouldn't one enjoy oneself in the bosom of one's family. I like to call him Malcolm Forde, it's such a pretty name; and one ought to get accustomed to the Christian name of one's future brother-in-law.'

Two of the Miss Luttrells flushed crimson at this speech: Gertrude, who turned angrily upon the speaker, as if about to retort; and Elizabeth, whose swift reply came like a flash of lightning, before her senior could reprove the offender.

'How dare you say that, Blanche? Do you suppose that I would marry Mr. Forde—a Curate—even if he were to ask me?'

'I won't suppose anything till he does ask you,' answered the incorrigible; 'and then I know pretty well what will happen. Whatever fine notions you may have had about a rich husband, and a house in London, and an opera-box, and goodness knows what, will all count for nothing the day that Malcolm Forde makes you an offer. Why, you worship the ground he walks on. Do you think we can't all of us see through your district-visiting? A pretty freak for you to take up, after admitting that you detested such work!'

'I suppose it is not quite unnatural that one should try to overcome one's dislikes, and to do some good in the world,' replied Elizabeth with dignity. 'Have the goodness to bridle your tongue a little, Blanche; and rest assured that I shall never marry a Curate, be he whom he may.'

'But Mr. Forde is not like common Curates. He is independent of the Church. He has private means.'

'Yes; three or four hundred a year from a small estate in Aberdeenshire.'

'O, you have been making inquiries, then?'

'No; but I heard papa say as much, one day. And now, Blanche, be so kind as to abandon the discussion of my affairs, and of Mr. Forde's, and let us talk of the picnic. I say Lawborough Beeches.'

This 'I say' was uttered in a tone of authority, unbefitting a third sister; and Gertrude immediately determined not to brook any such usurpation; but it somehow generally happened that Elizabeth had her own way. She had a happy knack of suggesting the right thing.

'Lawborough Beeches is a jolly place!' said Blanche approvingly.

'When will you learn to abandon the use of that odious adjective?' cried Gertrude with a shudder. 'Lawborough Beeches is low and damp.'

'Well, I'd as soon have it on the moor, and we could have donkey races and no end of fun.'

'Was there ever a girl with such vulgar ideas? Donkey races? Imagine Mr. Forde riding a donkey with a piece of white calico on its back! And imagine picnicking on the moor, without a vestige of shade! A nice blistered state our faces would be in! and I should have one of my nervous headaches,' said Diana, who had a kind of copyright in several interesting ailments of the nervine type.

Lawborough Beeches was a little wood of ancient trees, with silver-gray trunks and spreading crests; beeches which had been pollarded in the days when Cromwell rode rough-shod over the land, and had stretched out their mighty limbs low and wide in the centuries that had gone by since then. It was a little wood lying in a green hollow, through which

the Tabor meandered — a silvery stream dear to
the soul of the fly-fisher; here dark and placid
as a lake, under the broad shadow of the trees;
there flowing with swift current towards the distant
weir.

Miss Luttrell acknowledged somewhat unwill-
ingly, after a good deal of discussion, that the
Beeches was perhaps the best place for the picnic, if
the picnic were really a social necessity.

'I must confess that I do not see it in that light,'
she said, 'and I rather wonder that you should do
so, Elizabeth, now that your mind has been awakened to loftier interests. The sum which this picnic
will cost would be a great help to our blanket-club
next winter.'

Elizabeth pondered for a few moments. Of course
she was anxious to help those poor people who were
so fond of her; but the winter was a long way off.
Providence might increase her means in some un-
thought-of manner by that time. And the near delight of a long summer afternoon with Malcolm Forde
under Lawborough Beeches was very sweet to her.
She had seen so little of him of late. The very change
in herself, which she had fancied would bring them
nearer together, seemed to have only the more divided them. She did not meet him half so often as in

her unregenerate days, when she had been always
strolling in and out of Hawleigh, to change books at
the library; or to buy a new song, or a yard or two
of ribbon ; or to look at the last Paris fashions, which
the chief linendraper had just received—from Ply-
mouth.

'We ought to make some return for people's
hospitality,' she said. 'I consider the picnic un-
avoidable.'

So Blanche produced a sheet of foolscap, and began to make out a formidable list of comestibles :
pigeon-pies, chicken-salads, lobsters, plovers' eggs,
galantine of veal, hams, tongues, salmon *en mayon-
naise*, and so on, with a wild profusion that seems so
easy in pen-and-ink.

'I wish you would not be so officious, Blanche,'
exclaimed the eldest Miss Luttrell. 'Of course, I
shall arrange all those details with Susan Sims.'

Susan Sims was the cook—an important func-
tionary in the Vicar's household—who managed Miss
Luttrell.

'That means that we are to have whatever Susan
likes to give us !' said Blanche. 'You do give way
to her so, Gertrude. I think I'd rather have a bad
cook, and one's dinner spoilt occasionally, if one could
order just what one liked. However, I suppose, if I

mayn't make out a list of the dinner, I may make a
list of the people ?'

'Yes, you can, if you'll take your inkstand to another table. You've made a blot upon the table-cloth
already.'

Upon this, the three elder damsels separated to
pursue their divers occupations: Gertrude to hold
solemn converse with Susan Sims ; Diana to practise
Mendelssohn's sonatas on the drawing-room piano ;
Elizabeth to her district-visiting ; leaving Blanche
wallowing in ink, and swelling with importance, as
she wrote the names of her father's friends on two
separate sheets of foolscap—the people who must be
invited upon one, the people who might or might not
be invited upon the other.

Mr. Luttrell happened to be at home for luncheon
that day—a privilege which he was not permitted to
enjoy more than once or twice a week—so the sisters
were able to moot the question of the picnic without
delay.

The Vicar rubbed his bald forehead thoughtfully,
with a perplexed sigh.

'I suppose we must do something,' he said dolefully. 'It's a long time since we've had a dinner-
party; and if you think people really like their dinner
any better on damp grass, Gertrude, and with flies

dropping into their wine, why, have a picnic by all means. There's always an immense deal of wine drunk at these affairs, by the way; young men are so officious, and go opening bottles on the least provocation. Be sure you remind me to write and order some of the Ball-supper Champagne and the Racecourse Moselle we saw advertised the other day.'

The matter was settled, therefore, pleasantly enough, and the invitations were written that afternoon, and distributed before nightfall by the parsonage gardener or man-of-all-work, Mr. Forde's invitation among them; a formal little note in Gertrude's hand, which he twisted about in his fingers for a long time while he meditated upon his answer.

Would it do him any good to waste a summer day under Lawborough Beeches? He had been working his hardest for some weeks without relaxation of any kind. He felt that he wanted rest and ease; but hardly this species of recreation, which would involve a great deal of trouble; for he would be required to make himself agreeable to all manner of people—to carry umbrellas and camp-stools; to point out interesting objects in the landscape; to quote the county history—and, in fact, to labour assiduously for the pleasure of other people. Nor had he ever felt himself any the better for these rustic pleasures;

considerably the worse rather, especially when they were shared with Elizabeth Luttrell.

No; better to waste his day in utter loneliness on the moor, under the shadow of a mighty tor, with a book lying unread at his side. Better to give himself a pause of perfect rest, in which to think out the great problem of his life. For without inordinate self-esteem, Malcolm Forde was a man who deemed that his existence ought to be of some use to the world, that he was destined to fill some place in the scheme of creation. He felt that *al-fresco* banquetings and junketings were just the idlest, most worthless use that he could make of his rare leisure; and yet, with very human inconsistency, he wrote to Miss Luttrell next morning to accept her kind invitation.

CHAPTER IV.

'O you gods!
'Why do you make us love your goodly gifts,
And snatch them straight away? We, here below,
Recall not what we give, and therein may
Vie honour with yourselves.'

A PERFECT lull in the summer winds, a sultry silence in the air; Tabor lying stilly under the beeches, dark and polished as a mirror of Damascus steel, not a bulrush on its margent, not a lily trembling on its bosom. There seemed almost a profanity in happy talk and laughter in that silent wood, where the great beeches that were crop-eared by Cromwell spread their gnarled limbs under the hot blue sky.

Mr. Luttrell's party, however, do not pause in their mirth to consider the fitness of things. It boots not them to ask whether Lawborough Beeches be not a scene more suited to Miltonic musings than to the consumption of lobster-salad and galantine de veau. They ask each other for salt, and bread, and bitter ale, while the lark pierces the topmost heavens with purest melody. They set champagne corks fly-

ing against the giant beechen trunks. They revel in
clotted cream and syllabub, and small talk and flirtation, amidst the solemn shadows of that leafy dell;
and then, when they have spent nearly two hours in
a business-like absorption of solids and fluids, or in
playful trifling with the lightest of the viands, as the
case may be, the picnickers abandon the scene of the
banquet, and wander away in little clusters of three
or four, or in solitary couples, dispersing themselves
throughout the wood, nay even beyond, to a broad
stretch of rugged heath that borders it on one side,
or to the slope of a hill which shelters it on the other.
Some tempt the dangers of smooth-faced Tabor in
Fred Melvin's trim-built wherry, or in the punt which
has conveyed a brace of Oxonians, James and Horace
Elgood, the sons of one of the squires whose broad
pastures border the town of Hawleigh.

Mr. Melvin has been anxious that Elizabeth
should trust herself upon that silver flood.

'You know you're fond of boating,' he pleads;
' and if you haven't seen much of the Tabor this way,
it's worth your while to come. The banks are a picture—no end of flowers—"I know a bank whereon
the wild thyme grows," and that kind of thing. One
would think Shakespeare had taken his notion from
hereabouts.'

'As if the Avon had no thymy banks!' exclaimed Elizabeth contemptuously. 'I don't care about boating this afternoon, thank you, Mr. Melvin. I am going for a walk.'

She glanced at Malcolm Forde as she spoke, almost pleadingly, as if she would have said, Give me one idle hour of your life. They had sat far apart at the banquet, Gertrude having contrived to keep the Curate at her side; they had travelled from Hawleigh in different carriages, and had exchanged hardly half a dozen sentences up to this stage of the entertainment. It seemed to Elizabeth as if they were fated never to be together. Already she began to think the picnic a failure. 'I only wanted it for the sake of being with him,' she said to herself hopelessly.

And here was that empty-headed Fred Melvin worrying her to go in his boat, while Malcolm Forde stood by, leaning against the gray trunk of a pollard willow, listlessly gazing at the river, and said never a word.

'Let Forde punt you down the river as far as the weir,' cried one of the Oxonians, coming unconsciously to her relief. 'There's an empty punt lying idle yonder, the one that brought the Towers party; and Forde was one of the best punters at Oxford.'

Mr. Forde had gone up for his degree at a late

stage of his existence, after he left the army, and his repute was known to these youngsters.

'There's nothing like a punt in this kind of weather, Miss Luttrell,' said the Oxonian, as he rolled up his shirt-sleeves and prepared himself to convey a boatload of young ladies in voluminous muslin skirts; 'such a nice lazy way of getting along.'

He stood up high above his freight, plunged his pole deep into the quiet water, and skimmed athwart the river with a slow noiseless motion soothing to see upon a summer afternoon, while Elizabeth was silently blessing him.

Mr. Forde did at last awake from his reverie.

'Shall I get the punt?' he asked; 'and will you come?'

'I should like it of all things,' she answered gently. She was not going to hazard the loss of this perfect happiness by any ill-timed coquetry. Yes, it was perfect happiness to be with him. She acknowledged as much as that to herself, if she did not acknowledge any more.

'I suppose I think so much of him simply because he thinks nothing of me,' she said to herself musingly, while Mr. Forde had gone a little way down the bank to fetch the punt.

He came back presently, with his coat off and his

sleeves rolled up like the Oxonian's, skilfully navigating his rude bark with lengthy vigorous arms that had pulled in the university eight. It was the first time that Elizabeth had seen him on the river, and she wondered a little to find him master of this secular accomplishment. He brought the broad stem of the punt against the bank at her feet.

'Wouldn't your sister Blanche like to go with us?' he asked, looking round in quest of that young lady. But Blanche had gone off in the wherry with the Melvin set—Miss Pooley, the doctor's daughter; the Miss Cumdens, the rich manufacturer's daughters; Captain Danvers, and Mr. Pynsent. Shrill laughter sounded from the reedy shores beyond the sharp curve of the river. Even James Elgood's punt was out of sight. They had the river all to themselves. Utter loneliness seemed to have come upon the scene. The sound of that shrill laughter dwindled and died away, and these two stood alone in the sweet summer silence, between sunlight and shadow, on the brink of deep still Tabor.

Elizabeth lingered on the bank, doubtful whether it would not be the properer course to wait for some stray reveller to join them before she took her place in the boat. A *tête-à-tête* excursion with Mr. Forde would entail sundry lectures from Gertrude, a general sense of disapproval perhaps in her small world. But Malcolm Forde stretched out his strong arm and calmly handed her into the punt. It was quite a luxurious kind of boat, as punts go, provided with a red cushion on one of the broad clumsy seats, and a tin vessel for baling out unnecessary water.

She seated herself in the stern, and they drifted away slowly, softly over the still blue water. It was the first time they had been together, and alone, since the morning when she called upon him at his lodgings.

For some time there was silence, sweet silence, only broken by the hum of insect life around them, and the skylark's song in the clear vault above. The navigation of a punt is not a very difficult business; but it requires some attention, and Tabor's windings involved some small amount of care in the navigation. This made a fair excuse for Mr. Forde's silence, and Elizabeth was content—content to watch the dark thoughtful face, the firmly-cut profile, the deep gray eyes, grave almost to severity; content to ponder on his life, wondering if it were hard work and careful thought for others that had blanched the ruddier tints from his somewhat sunken cheek, or whether he was by nature pale; wondering if that grave dignity, which made him different from the common race of

curates, were an earnest of future eminence, if he
were verily born to greatness, and a bishopric awaiting him in the days to come; wondering idly about
this thing and that, her fancies playing round him,
like the flickering shadows on his figure as the boat
shot under the trees, and she supremely content to
be in his company. Perhaps, since she had more
than all a woman's faults and weaknesses, it may
have been some gratification to her to consider that
this boating excursion would occasion some jealous
twinges in the well-ordered mind of her eldest
sister.

'Gertrude has such a way of appropriating people,' she said to herself, 'and I really believe Mr.
Forde considers her a paragon.'

The navigation grew easier by and by, as Tabor
became less weedy. The banks, now high and broken,
now sloping gently, were rich in varying beauty; but
it was not of wild flowers or shivering rushes that
Elizabeth thought in that slow summer voyage. The
banks slid by like pictures gently shifting as she
looked; now a herd of lazy kine, fetlock deep in the
odorous after-math, and then a little copse of ancient
hawthorn, and then a silvery creek darkly shadowed
here and there by drooping willows that had grown
aslant the stream. She was faintly conscious of these

things, and felt a vague delight in them; but her thoughts were all of Malcolm Forde.

'Did you ever hear that story of Andrew Marvell's father?' he said at last, breaking that lazy silence which had seemed only a natural element of the warm summer afternoon. There was a straight stretch of water now before him; so he laid down his pole, and seated himself in the bows with a pair of sculls. 'He was a Hull man, you know, and a clergyman, and was going across the Humber to marry a couple in Lincolnshire. He was seized with a strange presentiment on stepping into the boat, and flung his walking-stick ashore, crying, "Ho, for heaven!" The presage was not a false one, for old Marvell was drowned. The story came into my mind just now, when we left the bank, and I couldn't help feeling that it would be a pleasant way of solving the problem of life to shoot mid-stream at random, crying out, "Ho, for heaven!" like that old puritan parson.'

'It would be very nice if heaven could be reached so easily,' said Elizabeth, who had a feeling that for her the pilgrimage from this world to a better one must needs be difficult. She had never yet felt herself heavenly minded; of the earth, earthy rather, with mundane longings for an opera-box and a barouche-and-pair.

'But I did not think you were tired of life, Mr. Forde,' she added, after a little pause.

'Not exactly tired, but at times perplexed. I sometimes doubt whether I am doing much good in Hawleigh—whether, indeed, I am doing anything that a man of less energy and ambition might not do just as well.'

'You feel like an eagle doing the work of a crow,' she answered, smiling. 'I can fancy that Hawleigh must seem a narrow field for you. When you have persuaded people to decorate the churches, and attend the early services, and taught the choir to sing a little better, and bought surplices for the boys, it seems as if there was nothing left for you to do. I should think in a populous seaport, now, where there are narrow streets and a great many wicked people, you would have a wider sphere.'

'There might be more to do in a place of that kind,' he said thoughtfully. 'It wouldn't seem quite so much like a gardener's work in a trim smooth garden, always going over the same flower-beds, dragging up a little weed here and there, or cutting a withered branch. But that is not my dream. The field of action that I have thought about and longed for lies far away from England.'

He was looking, not at Elizabeth, but above her

head, along the shining river, as if he did indeed with his bodily eyes behold that wider land, that distant world of which he spoke.

Elizabeth grew pale with horror.

'You surely don't mean that you have ever thought of turning missionary?' she exclaimed.

'That has been my thought sometimes, when my work here has seemed wasted labour.'

She was inexpressibly shocked. The very idea was disagreeable to her. There was even a kind of commonness, in her mind, in the image of a missionary. She imagined him a Low-Church person, not very far removed from a dissenter, a man who let his hair grow long and was indifferent as to the fashion of his garments; such a man as she had heard hold forth, in short trousers and thick boots, at a meeting for the propagation of the Gospel. She did not imagine that the commonness was in her own mind, which could not perceive the width and grandeur in that sublime idea of gathering all the nations into one flock. It had never occurred to her that South-Sea Islanders were of any importance in the scheme of creation, that university men in this privileged quarter of the globe owed any duty to dusky heathens dancing strange dances in distant groves of palm and breadfruit trees under a hot blue sky.

'O, I hope you would never think of such a desperate thing,' she said with a little piteous look that
touched him strangely. 'It seems a kind of moral
suicide.'

'Say rather a second birth,' he answered: 'the
beginning of a new and wider life—a life worth
living.'

'You must care very little for any one on this
side of the world, when you can talk so calmly of
going to the other.'

'I have very few to care for,' he replied gravely.
'My family ties are represented by a bachelor uncle
in Aberdeenshire—a grim old man, who farms a wild
sheep-walk of five thousand acres or so, and lives in
a lonely homestead, where he hears few sounds except
the lowing of his kine and the roar of the German
Ocean. I think I am just the right kind of man for
a missionary; and if you knew the story of my life,
and the circumstance that led to my change of profession, I fancy you would agree with me.'

'But I know nothing of your life,' Elizabeth cried
impatiently. She was unreasonably angry with him
for this missionary project, almost as angry as if it
had been a deliberate wrong done to herself. 'You
came to us a stranger, and you have remained a
stranger to us, though you have been at Hawleigh

more than a year. You are so reserved—not like papa's other curates, who were only too glad to pour out their inmost feelings, as it were. I'm sure I knew every detail of Mr. Dysart's family—his papa's opinions, his mamma's little peculiarities, the colour of all his sisters' hair, even the history of the gentlemen to whom the sisters were engaged. And it was almost the same with Mr. Horton. Mr. Adderley was fonder of prosing about himself than his surroundings, and I don't think the poor young man ever had an idea in his rather narrow brain that he did not impart to us.'

'You see I am not of so communicative a disposition,' said Mr. Forde, smiling; 'and when there has been one great sorrow in a life, as there has in mine, it is apt to assume an unnatural proportion to the rest, and obscure all minor details. I had a great loss five years before I came to Hawleigh. I have often been inclined to tell you all about it, especially of late, since I have seen your character in its most amiable light. But these things are painful to speak of, and my loss was a very bitter one.'

'You are speaking of the death of your mother?' inquired Elizabeth, trembling a little, with a strange sharp dread.

'No; my mother died fifteen years ago. That

loss was bitter, but it was one for which I had been long prepared. The later loss was utterly unexpected, and shattered the very fabric of my life.'

'I should like to hear about it,' said Elizabeth, her face bent over the water, one idle hand drawn loosely through the tide.

'I am assured that you are kind and sympathetic,' he said, 'or I should never have touched upon this subject. I never had a sister, and perhaps on that account have not acquired the habit of confession. But—but—' very slowly, and with a curious hesitation, 'I think I should like to talk to you—about her. About Alice Fraser, the woman who was to have been my wife.'

The face bent over the river flushed crimson, the little white hand shivered in the tide; but Elizabeth spoke no word.

'When I went to India with my regiment—it was just after the Mutiny—I left my promised wife behind me. We were old friends, had been playfellows even, though the little Scottish lassie was seven years younger than I. She was the daughter of a Scotch parson, a man of noble mind and widest reading, and the best friend and counsellor I ever had. I will not try to tell you what she was like. To me she seemed perfection, pretty enough to be charming, full of brightness and vivacity, yet with a depth and earnestness in her nature that made me —her senior by seven years—feel that here was a staff to lean upon through all the journey of life. I cannot tell you how I revered this girl of nineteen. You will think perhaps that she was self-opinionated, or what people call strong-minded; but there was never a more simple unassuming nature. She had been educated by her father, and on a wider plan than the common scheme of a woman's teaching. Of late years she had shared his studies, and had been his chosen companion in every hour of leisure. Of her goodness to the people round about her I cannot trust myself to speak. Her memory is cherished in Lanorgie as the memory of a saint. I doubt if, among all who knew her well in that simple flock, there is one who could speak of her even now without tears.'

He paused for some few minutes, perhaps lost in thought, recalling that remote Scottish village, and the sweet girlish face that had been the light of his life six years ago. The oars dipped gently in the river, the boat glided onward with imperceptible motion, and Elizabeth sat silent with her face still bent over the water, dragging the long green river-weeds through her cold white fingers.

'She had the very slightest Scottish accent—an

accent that gave a plaintive tone to her voice, like
music in a minor key. She was slender and fragile,
just about the middle height, very fair but very pale,
with soft brown hair—the sort of woman a painter
would choose for Imogen or Ophelia; not an objective
nature, strongly marked with its own individuality;
subjective rather, yet strong enough to resist all evil.
A bad husband might have broken her heart; but he
would never have sullied her mind.'

He stopped again, laid down his sculls, and drew
the boat under the reedy bank. Elizabeth was obliged to look up now. The little gray straw hat with
its convenient shadow hid the change in her face, in
some measure; but not entirely, for Mr. Forde observed that she was very pale.

'I fear you are tired,' he said, 'or that my dreary
talk has wearied you.'

'No, no; go on. She must have been very good.'

'She had less of humanity's alloy than any creature I ever knew,' he answered. 'I used to think
that it would be a privilege for any man—the best
even—to spend his life in her company. There was
one subject that gave her great pain, and that was
the fact of my profession. To her gentle spirit there
was something horrible in a soldier's career. She
could not see the nobler side of my calling. And I

loved her too well to hold by anything that gave her pain. I promised her that I would sell out immediately on my return from foreign service, and I kept my word.'

'It was not of your own accord, then, that you left the army?' asked Elizabeth absently, as if only half her brain were following his words.

'No; it was entirely to please Alice. I sacrificed my own inclinations in the matter. That conviction which has become the very keystone of my life since then is a faith that grew out of my great sorrow. I cannot tell you the rest of the story too briefly. I went back to Lanorgie a free man. I was to be a farmer —a country gentleman on a small scale—anything Alice pleased, in the district where I was born. My sweet girl was to live for ever among the people she loved. Our life was to be Arcadian—a pastoral poem. We were both very happy. I can safely declare that there was not left in my mind one spark of mankind's common desire of success or distinction. The long calm years stretched themselves out before me in sweet eventless happiness.'

'You must have loved her very much?'

'If you could measure my love by the change it made in me, you would have good reason to say so. I had been as eager as other young men for name, position, wealth, pleasure—perhaps even more eager. But Alice's love filled my mind with a great content. She made herself the sum of my life. I desired nothing beyond the peaceful circle of the home that she and I were to share together. Well, Miss Luttrell,'—this with a sudden abruptness, as if the words were wrenched from him,—' it was a common trouble enough when it came. Our wedding-day was fixed; her old father—every one was happy. The last touch had been put to our new home; a house I had built for my darling upon a hill-side facing the sea, on my own land. Everything was arranged—our honeymoon trip southwards to the Cumberland lakes had been planned between us on the map one sweet summer evening. We parted at her father's door; she a little graver than usual—but that seemed natural on the threshold of so great a change. When I went to the manse next morning, they told me she was not quite well—that her father's old friend, the village doctor, recommended her to keep her room for a day or two, and to see no one. She had had a little too much excitement and fatigue lately. I reproached myself bitterly for our long walks on the hills and by the rugged sea-shore we both loved so well. All she wanted was perfect rest.

' They kept me off like this for nearly a week;

now confessing reluctantly that she was not quite so well; now cheering me with the assurance that she was better. Then one morning I heard they had sent to Glasgow for a physician. After that, I insisted upon seeing her.

'She did not know me. I stood beside her bed, and the sweet blue eyes looked up at me, but she was unconscious. The physician acknowledged that it was a case of typhoid fever. There was very little ground for hope. Yet we did hope—blindly—to the last. I telegraphed for other doctors. But we could not save her. She died in my arms at daybreak on the day that was to have seen us married.

'I will not speak of the dead blank that followed her death—of the miserable time in which I could think of nothing but the one fact of my loss. The time came at last when I could think of her more calmly, and then I set myself to consider what I could do, now she was gone, to prove that I had loved her—what tribute I could render to my dead. It was then I thought of entering the Church—of devoting myself, so far as in me lay, to the good of others—of leading such a life as she would have blessed. That is the origin of all I have done, of all I hope to do. That is the end of my story, Miss Luttrell. I trust I have not tired you very much. I thought we should be better friends, if you knew more about my past.'

'I am very glad,' she answered gently. 'I have sometimes fancied there must be something in your life, some sorrowful memory: not that there has ever seemed anything gloomy in your character; but you are so much more in earnest, altogether so unlike papa's other curates.'

A faint blush lit up the pale face as she said this, remembering that he differed most widely from these gentlemen in his total inability to appreciate herself.

Yes, she had fancied there was some bitter memory in his past, but not this. His confidence had strangely shocked her. It was inexpressibly painful to her to discover that his love—and so profound a love—had all been lavished upon another woman years ago; that were she, Elizabeth Luttrell, twice as lovely, twice as fascinating as she was, she could never be anything to him. He had chosen his type of womanly perfection; he had given away all the feeling, all the passion that it was in him to give, long before he had seen her face.

'Did he suppose that—that I was beginning to think too much of him,' she said to herself, blushing indignantly, 'and tell me this story by way of a warning? O, no, no! his manner was too straightforward for that. He thinks that I am good, thinks that I am able to sympathise with him, to pity him, to be sorry for that dead girl. And I am not. I think I am jealous of her in her grave.'

The boat glides softly on. They come to a curve of the river, and to Mr. Melvin's party returning noisily.

'You are not going to take Miss Elizabeth any farther, are you?' cries Frederick. 'We are going back to tea. How slow you've been! We went as far as the Bells, and had some shandy-gaff.'

Mr. Forde turned his clumsy bark, and all the voyage back was noisy with the talk of the Melvin party and the Oxonians' punt-load of vivacious humanity. They were all in holiday spirits, laughing on the faintest provocation, at the smallest imaginable jokes. Elizabeth thought it the most dismal business. All the sunshine was taken out of her afternoon; Tabor seemed a sullen stream flowing between flat weedy banks. But she could not afford to let other people perceive her depression—Mr. Forde above all. She was obliged to affect amusement at those infinitesimal jokes, those stale witticisms, while she was thinking all the time of that thrice-blessed woman whom Malcolm Forde had loved, and who had timely died while his passion was yet in its first bloom and freshness.

'I daresay if she had gone on living he would have been tired of her by this time,' she said to herself in a cynical mood. 'She would have been his wife of ever so many years' standing, with a herd of small children, perhaps, on her mind, and just as commonplace as all the wives one knows—women whose intellects hardly soar above nursemaids and pinafores. How much better to be a sacred memory all his life than a prosaic fact in his everyday existence!'

After this, Elizabeth felt as if she could have no more pleasure in Malcolm Forde's society. Her selfish soul revolted against the idea that the memory of his dead was more to him than any favour her friendship could bestow, that she was divided from him by the width of a grave.

'I wish his Alice had lived, and he stayed among his native hills with the rest of the Scotch barbarians,' she said to herself. 'I don't think I've been quite happy since I've known him. He makes one feel such a contemptible creature, with his grand ideas of what a woman ought to be; and then, after one has tried one's hardest to be good against one's very nature, he coolly informs one that there never was but one perfect woman in the world, and that she lies among the Scottish hills with his heart buried in her grave.'

CHAPTER V.

' Well, you may, you must, set down to me
    Love that was life, life that was love ;
A tenure of breath at your lips' decree,
    A passion to stand as your thoughts approve,
    A rapture to fall where your foot might be.'

THE gipsy-tea went off brilliantly. The fuel-col-
lecting and fire-making and kettle-boiling afforded
ample sport for those wilder and more youthful spirits
whose capacity for flirtation was not yet exhausted.
Fred Melvin belonged to that harmless class of young
men who, although in the dull round of daily life but
moderately gifted, shine forth with unexpected lustre
on such an occasion as this, and prove themselves
what their friends call 'an acquisition.' He fanned
life and light into a hopelessly obstinate fire, with
his straw-hat for an extemporaneous bellows; he
showed a profound knowledge of engineering in his
method of placing the kettle on the burning logs, so
as not immediately to extinguish the flames he had
just coaxed into being.

    ' I don't think there was anything so very wonder-

ful in Watt inventing the steam-engine,' said Miss
Melvin, standing by and admiring her brother's dex-
terity; 'I believe Fred would have been quite as
likely to hit upon it, if it hadn't been done before his
time.'

They drank tea in little scattered groups: the
elders foregathering in small knots to talk scandal or
parish business, or to indulge in mild jeremiads upon the frivolity and general empty-headedness of the
rising generation, their own sons and daughters and
nephews and nieces not excepted; the juniors to dis-
port themselves after their kind with inexhaustible
nothings, vapid utterances which filled the soul of
Elizabeth with contempt.

She carried her tea-cup away to a lonely little bit
of bank where the rushes on the shelving shore grew
high enough to screen her from the rest of the company, and sat here alone, absorbed in languid contemplation of the quiet water and all the glories of
the sunset reflected on that smooth tide.

Fred Melvin, seeing the white dress vanishing
beyond the trees, would fain have gone in pursuit,
but the Luttrell sisters prevented him.

'Elizabeth has one of her headaches, I daresay,'
said Diana. 'It would be no use going after her.'

'One of her tempers, you mean, Di,' exclaimed

Blanche with sisterly candour. 'That's always the way with Lizzie if everything doesn't happen exactly as she wants it to happen. I think she would like a world made to order, on purpose for her.'

'I hope we haven't done anything to offend her,' cried the anxious Frederick, whose adoration of 'the Beauty,' as chief goddess of his soul, had never suffered diminution, not even when he amused himself by offering his homage at lesser shrines. 'Perhaps she didn't like our going off in the boat without her; but it really couldn't have held so much as a lap-dog beyond our load.'

'As if anything *you* could do would offend her!' exclaimed the impetuous Blanche, always ready to rebuke Mr. Melvin's vain passion. 'Do you think she wanted to come in our boat? She would have given her ears for that *tête-à-tête* row with Mr. Forde, only I suppose it didn't answer.'

'Blanche, how can you be so absurd!' cried Gertrude.

'If you don't learn to behave yourself with common decency, we really must leave you at home in the nursery another time,' said Diana.

Mr. Forde was happily beyond the hearing of this little explosion. He was in infinite request among the matrons of the party, who all regarded

him more or less as a modern St. Francis de Sales,
and who gave him not a little trouble by their insistence upon communicating small facts relating to
their spiritual progress; little sentimental gushes of
feeling which he did his best to check, his ideas of
his duty being of the broadest and grandest character.
He would rather have had the conversion of all the
hardened or remorseful felons at Portland or Dartmoor on his hands than these gushing matrons and
sentimental spinsters, who could not travel the
smallest stage of their journey towards the heavenly
Jerusalem without being propped and sustained by
him.

Nor was it pleasant to listen to little laments
about the Vicar. 'A kind generous-minded man, Mr.
Forde, and very good to the poor, I believe, in his
own careless way,—but so unspiritual! We hardly
knew what light was till you came among us.' And
so on, and so on. He was glad to slip away from the
elder tea-drinkers, and stroll in and out among the
giant beech boles, with the gay sound of youthful
laughter and happy idle talk filling the atmosphere
around him.

He lingered to say a few words to Gertrude Luttrell and her party, and then looked round the circle
curiously, as if missing some one.

'I don't see your sister,' he said at last, 'Miss Elizabeth.'

Miss Luttrell coloured furiously.

'Lizzie has strayed off somewhere,' she said. 'She appears to prefer the company of her own thoughts to *our* society. Perhaps had she known you would express so much anxiety about her, she would have stayed.'

'I am not particularly anxious,' replied Mr. Forde, with his thoughtful smile, a smile which lent sudden life and brightness to the dark grave face. 'Only I have it on my conscience that I kept your sister on the river a long while under a blazing sun, and I feared she might be too tired to enjoy herself with the rest of you. Can I take her a cup of tea?'

'I don't think I would if I were you,' cried Fred Melvin, who was in a picturesque attitude, half kneeling, half reclining at the feet of Blanche Luttrell, while his cousin Jane Harrison, for whom there was some dim notion of his ripening into a husband by and by, sat looking on with an aggrieved air. 'I took her a second cup just now,' grumbled Fred, 'and very nearly got my nose snapped off for my pains.'

Not an encouraging statement; but Mr. Forde was not afraid of any attacks upon his nose: was not that feature in a manner sanctified by his profession, and the very high rate at which the curate race is held two hundred and fifty miles from London ? He was in nowise deterred by Mr. Melvin's plaint, but went off at once in quest of Elizabeth.

'I saddened her with that melancholy story,' he thought. 'Perhaps I ought not to have told her. Yet I think she is the kind of woman a man might dare to choose out of all other women for his friend. I think she is of a different stuff from the rest of Hawleigh womankind. She has shown herself superior to them all in her power to win the love of the poor. And we could never be friends until she knew my story, and knew that the word "love" has been blotted from the book of my life.'

It was a new fancy of Mr. Forde's, this desire that there should really be friendship—something more than the every-day superficial acquaintance engendered by church decoration and croquet—between himself and Elizabeth Luttrell. It was not to be in the slightest degree sentimental—the popular platonic idea. The Madame-Récamier-and-Chateaubriand kind of thing had never entered into his thoughts, nor did he mean that they should see any more of each other than they had done heretofore ; only that there should be confidence and trust between them instead of strangeness.

He found her presently on her lonely bank by the Tabor, seated in a thoughtful attitude, and casting little turfs of moss and lady's-slipper idly upon the tide. She had arrayed herself with a studied simplicity for this rustic gathering; perhaps fully conscious that she was one of the few women who can afford to dispense with frillings and puffings and ruchings— the whole framework of beauty, as it were. She wore a plain white-muslin gown, high to the throat, round which she had tied a dark-blue ribbon—the true Oxford blue, almost black against the ivory-white of her neck. The long dark ribbon made a rippling line to the perfect waist; perfect in its exquisite proportion to the somewhat full and stately figure—the waist of a Juno rather than a sylph. Her head was uncovered, and the low sunlight lit up all the bronze tints in her dark-brown hair, shone, too, in the luminous gray eyes, fixed dreamily upon the gleaming water. Mr. Forde stood for a few moments a little way off, admiring her—simply as he would have admired a picture, of course.

His footsteps made a faint rustling among the rushes as he came nearer to her. She looked round suddenly, and all her face flushed crimson at sight of him.

That blush would have elevated Fred Melvin to the seventh heaven; but Malcolm Forde was no coxcomb, and did not attribute the heightened tint to any magical power of his own. She was nervous, perhaps, and he had startled her by his sudden approach; or she might be indeed, as her friends had suggested, a little out of temper, and annoyed at being tracked to her lair.

'Don't be angry with me for disturbing your solitary musings, Miss Elizabeth,' he said, very much detesting the ceremonial Miss; 'but I really don't think you're enjoying your father's picnic quite so much as you ought, for your own satisfaction and that of your friends.'

'I hate picnics,' she answered peevishly; 'and if papa gives one next year, I'll have nothing to do with it. I'm sure I wish I'd stayed in Hawleigh and gone to see my poor people. I should have been much happier sitting by Mrs. Jones's wash-tub, or reading to Mrs. Brown while she mended her husband's stockings.'

'If you speak like that, I shall think I spoiled your pleasure by that egotistical talk in the boat.'

She only shook her head and looked away from

him at a distant curve of the river. There was an awkward sensation of semi-strangulation in her throat. For her very life she could not have answered him. Yes, it was a bitter disappointment to discover that he had flung away his heart before he came to Hawleigh; that he was a kind of widower, and pledged never to marry again.

'I am so sorry that I told you that story. Of course it was no fitting time. I was a brute not to have thought of that; but we so rarely have time for a confidential talk, and I have been so much interested in your work lately, so much pleased by your hearty manner of taking up a duty which I know did at first seem uncongenial to you, and I was anxious that we should be friends. Pray do not let the gloom of my past life weigh upon your spirits even for an hour. It was a most ill-advised confession. Try to forget that it was ever made.'

Silence still, and the head turned obstinately towards the river. Was it temper? or compassion for another's woes more profound than he had dreamed of?

' Say, at least, that you forgive me for having depressed you.'

Still no answer in words, but a hand stretched out towards his, a hand chill as death.

'Let me take you back to your friends,' he said, alarmed by the cold touch of that little hand, which he clasped for a moment with a friendly pressure and then let fall. 'I shall not forgive myself till I see you happy with the others.'

She rose slowly and took the arm which he offered her. That choking sensation had been conquered by this time, and she was able to answer him quite calmly.

'Pray don't distress yourself about me,' she said; 'I am very glad that you told me your story, that you think me worthy of your confidence.'

He took her back to the circle under the Beeches. Cups and saucers were being gathered up, the bustle of preparation for departure had begun. Wagonette, omnibus, and dogcart stood ready for the homeward journey, and the usual discussions and disputes as to the mode and manner of return were going on: elderly spinsters languishing to travel on the roof of the omnibus, and protesting their affection for the perfume of cigars; fastish young ladies pleading for the same privilege; and all the male kind thinly disguising the leaven of selfishness that was in them, and their desire to appropriate the roof to their own accommodation, by an affected solicitude as to the hazard of cold-catching.

'We ought to have had a dance,' grumbled Blanche; 'it would have been the easiest thing in the world to bring a couple of men with a harp and a fiddle, but I suppose it would have been considered unclerical. It would have been so nice. We should have fancied ourselves fairies tripping lightly under the greenwood tree. I declare it seems quite a shame to go home so early—just when the air is pleasantest, and all the stars are beginning to peep out of their nests in the sky—as if we were a children's tea-party.'

The fiat, however, had gone forth, the vehicles were ready, the fogy-ish element in the party eager to depart before dews began to fall, and toads, bats, owls, spiders, and other rustic horrors to pervade the scene; the juvenile population loath to go, yet eager for the excitement of the return journey, with all its opportunities for unlimited flirtation.

Fred Melvin was the proud proprietor of the dog-cart, a conveyance usually appropriated to the uses of his father—the family carriage, in short—which, if it had only possessed one of those removable American-oven tops popular in the rural districts, would have even done duty for a brougham. Urged thereto by his sister, and with considerable reluctance, the young solicitor entreated Mr. Forde, who had come on the box of the omnibus, to accept a seat in his chariot—a variety in the mode of return being esteemed a privilege by the picnickers.

'Mr. Forde won't want to go back on the omnibus, I daresay, Fred,' argued Laura Melvin. 'You might as well offer him a seat in the dogcart.'

To which suggestion Frederick growled that he wanted no parsons, and that he was going to ask one of the Luttrell girls.

'You can ask one of the Miss Luttrells, too, Fred. There'll only be you and me and Mr. Forde. Jenny's going home inside the omnibus. She has a touch of her neuralgia; and I don't wonder, poor girl, you've been flirting so shamefully with Blanche Luttrell. I wonder how a girl hardly out of pinafores can go on so.'

So Fred went away to offer the vacant seats; first to Mr. Forde, with reluctant politeness.

'You don't like too much smoke, I daresay, and those fellows on the 'bus will be smoking like so many factory chimneys every inch of the way. You'd better have your quiet cigar in my trap.'

'You're very good. I don't like bad tobacco, certainly; and the odours I enjoyed coming were not by any means the perfumes of Arabia. But are you sure I shall not be in the way?'

' O, you won't be in the way. I am going to ask Lizzie Luttrell, and that'll make up the four.'

Mr. Forde winced at this familiar mention of the damsel in whom he had permitted himself to become interested; but that kind of familiarity is a natural attribute of brothers in their intercourse with their sisters' friends. 'A different race, these provincial brothers, from the rest of mankind,' Mr. Forde thought.

' I'm going to ask her,' repeated Frederick, as he tightened the chestnut mare's kicking-strap, ' but I don't suppose she'll come, unless her temper's undergone some improvement since I took her that cup of tea.'

Elizabeth Luttrell drew nigh at this moment, in grave converse with a little silver-headed gentleman, the ancient banker of Hawleigh.

To Mr. Melvin's surprise, she accepted his offer with extreme graciousness.

' I like a dogcart above all things,' she said, ' especially if I may sit behind. I do so like the excitement of the sensation that one will be jerked off if the horse shies.'

But against this Fred protested vehemently.

' You must sit next the driver,' he said; ' Laura

can sit behind with Mr. Forde. Not that Bess ever shies, but you must have the post of honour.'

'Then I'll go home in the omnibus,' said Lizzie; 'I know riding behind always makes Laura nervous.'

Miss Melvin, pressed hard upon this point, acknowledged that the jerky sensation which was pleasant to Elizabeth's bolder spirit was eminently appalling to herself. So Elizabeth had her own way, and occupied the back seat of the dogcart, with Mr. Forde by her side.

The journey back to Hawleigh was a ten-mile drive through west-country lanes, bordered by steep banks and tall tangled hedges that shut out the land-scape, except for those privileged travellers on the roof of the omnibus. Only now and then did the dogcart emerge from the shadow of hawthorn and woodbine, wild rose and wild apple, into the moon-lit open country; but the odour of those leafy lanes was sweet, and beyond them, far away in the soft silver light, spread fair hill-sides and wooded slopes, and brief flashes of the winding river.

It only lasted an hour and a quarter, that home-ward journey, the dogcart keeping well ahead of the heavier vehicles, and Bess the mare performing the distance in so superior a manner as almost to justify that pride in her which was one of the chief articles of faith in the household code of the Melvins. Elizabeth would have thought better of the animal had she loitered a little on the way. Not often could she enjoy a moonlight *tête-à-tête* with Mr. Forde—for it mattered little that Fred interjected his trivial little remarks every now and then across Miss Luttrell's shoulder; not often had he unbent to her as he unbent to-night, talking to her as if she were verily in some measure a part of his inner life, and not a mere accident in the outer world around him. That confession of his past sorrows seemed really to have brought them a little closer together, and Elizabeth began to think there might indeed be such a thing as friendship between them; friendship that would brighten the dull round of district-visiting, sweeten all her life, and yet leave her free to dream her favourite day-dream of a wealthy marriage in the days to come; a splendid position won suddenly by her beauty; a swift and easy translation to a land flowing with silks and laces and all kinds of Parisian millinery; a little heaven here below in the way of opera-boxes and races and flower-shows and morning concerts; while Mr. Forde remained at liberty to fulfil that scheme of a monkish life which he had in his own quiet manner avowed to his more familiar friends of the district-visiting class.

'And perhaps some day, after I am married, he will really go to the South-Sea Islands, or the centre of Africa, as a missionary,' she thought, with a little regretful sigh; 'and years afterwards, when I am middle-aged and his hair is growing gray, he will come back to England as Bishop of Tongataboo, or some fearful place, and I shall hear him preach a charity sermon at a fashionable London church.'

It seemed hardly worth her while to be sorry about so remote a contingency; but she could not help feeling a pang at the thought that this part of her vision was the most likely to be realised: that whether the hypothetical baronet, with thirty thousand a year, did or did not appear upon the narrow scene of her life, Malcolm Forde would spread his pinions and soar away to a wider field than this small provincial town.

The dogcart arrived at the gate of Hawleigh Vicarage quite half an hour in advance of the other vehicles. It was past ten o'clock, and rare lights burned dimly in the upper casements of the houses that were scattered here and there along the highroad on this side of the town, the more exclusive and suburban quarter, adorned by the trim gothic lodges of the villas that half aspired to be country seats. The vicarage servants—Ann the sometime nurse and general factotum, Susan the cook, Rebecca the housemaid, and Jakes the man-of-all-work—were clustered at the gate, waiting to witness the return of the picnickers, as more sophisticated domestics might stand at gaze to see all the drags and wagonettes and hansom cabs of the famous Derby pilgrimage file slowly past Clapham-common.

'You'll come in, won't you, Laura?' said Elizabeth, who did not wish her evening to close abruptly with brief farewells at the gate. 'Jakes can take care of your horse, Mr. Melvin. You'll wait for papa, won't you, Mr. Forde, and to say good-night to every one?'

'If you are sure that you are not tired, and would be glad to get rid of us and go in and rest,' said Mr. Forde doubtfully.

'I am not in the least tired. I feel more in the humour to begin a picnic than I did at one o'clock to-day. Why, in London fashionable people are only just beginning to go out to parties! We seem to cut off the best end of our lives in the country with our stupid humdrum habits. Don't you think the night is best, Mr. Forde?'

'For study, I admit.'

'O, for pleasure, for everything!' cried Elizabeth impatiently. 'I feel another creature at night, out of doors, in summer moonlight like this. There is

a kind of intoxication : one's soul seems to soar away
into clearer air, into dreamland.   What would dancing be like at eleven o'clock in the morning, or at
three on a sultry afternoon ?   Why, it would seem
perfect lunacy !   But at night, with open windows,
and the moonlight outside, and the scent of the
flowers blowing in from the garden, it is simply rapture, because we are not quite the same people, you
see, towards midnight.   For my own part, on a summer evening I always feel as if I had wings.'   She
said this in a rapid excited tone, as if this particular
moonlight had indeed produced an abnormal effect
upon her spirits.

They had all strolled into the garden, Frederick
having reluctantly committed the mare to the man-
of-all-work.   Mr. Forde was walking between the two
young ladies, Miss Melvin feeling that it was mere
foolishness to hope for any attention from a curate
while Elizabeth ran on in that wild and almost dis-
reputable way of hers, not in the least like a well-
brought-up young lady.   But then it was a well-
known fact that the Luttrell girls had received only
a desultory training, not the regular old-established
boarding-school grinding : but sometimes a morning
governess, and sometimes an interregnum of inter-
mittent instruction from their father ; sometimes

masters for music and drawing, sometimes nothing at all. They were all clever girls, of course, said the genteel matrons of Hawleigh, or they could hardly have grown up as well as they had; but they had not enjoyed the advantages of the orthodox discipline for the youthful mind, and the consequences of this irregular education cropped up occasionally. The girls had read almost what they liked, and had stronger opinions than were becoming in a vicar's daughters.

To Laura Melvin's gratified surprise, Mr. Forde did not take any notice of Elizabeth's tirade about moonlight, but turned to her, Laura, and began to question her politely respecting her enjoyment of the day, while Fred, eager to snatch his opportunity, flew to Elizabeth.

'Didn't Bess do the ten miles well?' he asked by way of a lively beginning, quite prepared to have his advances ill received.

But Elizabeth was still under the intoxication of the moonlight. She was a person of singularly variable spirits, and the sullen gloom that had come upon her after that interview in the boat had now changed to a reckless vivacity.

'The drive was delightful,' she said. 'I should like to scamper all over Devonshire and Cornwall in such a dogcart, with just such a horse, stopping at

all manner of wild places, and being benighted, and
camping on the moors.   What a mistake it is to live
all one's life shut up between four walls, in the same
place, with no more variety from year's end to year's
end than a fortnight in seaside lodgings!   O, how I
wish Providence had made me a gipsy, or a Bedouin
Arab!'

'Awfully jolly, I should think, the Bedouins,'
replied Fred doubtfully.   'They tumble, don't they?
I remember seeing some Bedouin tumblers at Vaux-
hall when I was a youngster, and was up in London
with the paternal party.   But those were all men and
boys.   I don't think the women tumbled; and *their*
lives must have been uncommonly dull, shut up somewhere in London lodgings, while their husbands and
brothers were performing, not being able to speak
English, you know, poor creatures, or anything.'

'O you stupid Fred!' cried Elizabeth, who sometimes deigned to address the young man in this
familiar way.   'As if I meant performing Arabs!   I
should like to be the daughter of some Arab chief in
the great desert, with my own darling horse to carry
me on the wings of the wind, and only a tent to live
in, and locusts and wild honey for my dinner, like
John the Baptist.   I should like to be one of those
nice brown-faced girls who go about the country with

a van-load of mats and brooms. There seems something respectable in brooms. They would hardly send me to prison as a rogue and vagabond; and O, how nice it must be never to stay very long in the same place!'

'And to have no friends and no home, and no books or piano, and to be of no particular use in the world; only always toiling more or less hopelessly for one's daily bread; and to die some day by the roadside, of hard work and exposure to all kinds of weather,' continued Mr. Forde, who had soon exhausted his little stock of civilities to Miss Melvin, and turned to listen to Elizabeth's random talk. 'I'm afraid you must be very tired of us all, Miss Luttrell, when your soul yearns for the broom-girl life.'

'Not so tired as you confess yourself to be of *us* when you contemplate converting the heathen,' answered the girl, turning her back upon the hapless Frederick.

'It is not because I am tired of you that I think sometimes of a broader field and harder work,' he answered gravely, 'but for quite a different reason—because I sometimes find my life here too easy, too pleasant; an enervating life, in short. It is not always wise for a man to trust himself to be happy.'

'I thought you had done with happiness, after—

what you told me this afternoon,' said Elizabeth, almost bitterly.

Her speech shocked him a little. He answered it
in his coldest tones.

'With one kind of happiness, yes, and that per-
·haps the only perfect happiness in this world—companionship with a perfect woman.'

'A very good way of reminding me that I'm an
imperfect one,' thought Elizabeth, not unconscious
of deserving the implied rebuke.

They walked slowly round the garden in the moonlight, side by side, but somewhat silent after this,
leaving Frederick to straggle in their rear with his
sister, an ignominious mode of treatment which he
inwardly resented. Nor was he sorry when the omnibus and wagonette drove up to the gate to release
him from this humiliating position. He felt himself
rehabilitated in his own self-esteem when Blanche,
who really came next to Elizabeth in the scale of
prettiness, skipped gaily up to him, telling him that
she had had the dullest imaginable drive inside the
omnibus, and that she had been dreadfully jealous of
Lizzie, who of course had been having capital fun in
the dogcart.

'I don't know whether Forde is particularly good
fun,' Mr. Melvin replied with a sulky air. 'Your

sister had *him* all to herself. There was no getting in a word edgeways. I think when a man as good as gives out from the pulpit that he never means to marry, he ought to give up flirting into the bargain.'

'O Fred, how shameful of you to say such a thing! As if Mr. Forde ever flirted!'

'I should like to know what he's doing now,' grumbled Fred. 'If that isn't the real thing, it's an uncommonly good imitation.'

Elizabeth had taken up her favourite position by the sundial, and Malcolm Forde was standing by her, talking earnestly, or at least with an appearance of earnestness; and it is one of the misfortunes of youth that two persons of opposite sex cannot converse for ten minutes with any show of interest without raising suspicions of flirtation in the minds of the beholders.

'Doesn't it seem absurd,' exclaimed the aggrieved Frederick, 'after all Elizabeth has said about never marrying a clergyman?'

'She's not obliged to marry Mr. Forde because she talks to him for five minutes, is she, you stupid creature?' cried Blanche, disapproving this appearance of concern in her admirer—eligible young men were so rare at Hawleigh.

And now, after some consumption of claret-cup or sherry-and-soda among the elders in the low candle-lit drawing-room, and a little straggling flirtation among the juniors here and there about the garden, there came a general good-night, and Mr. Luttrell's guests dispersed, in carriages or on foot, to that gentleman's supreme contentment. This kind of thing was one of the penalties that went along with a flock of daughters.

'Thank heaven, that's over,' he said with a faint groan, and in a tone of voice strangely different from the friendly warmth of his last farewell. 'And now mind, I am not to be bothered about any more party-giving on this side of Christmas.'

'I am sure I shouldn't care if there were never to be another party on the face of the earth,' said Elizabeth drearily. Whereby it might be supposed that, so far as the prettiest Miss Luttrell was concerned, the day's festivities had been a failure.

Blanche questioned her by and by up in their tower chamber—the ancient octagon room, with its deep-set casements and litter of girlish trifles, its bird-cages and book-shelves, and glove-boxes and scent-bottles—questioned her closely, but at the outset could extort very little from those firm proud lips.

'You know you were glad to have that drive home with him,' said the girl persistently. 'You know you quarrelled with him in the boat, and were miserable afterwards. You know you are fond of him, Lizzie. What's the good of trying to hide it from me?'

'Fond of him!' cried Elizabeth passionately. 'Fond of a man who scarcely ever says a civil word to me! Fond of a man who, if he ever were to care for me—and he never will—would want to make me a district-visitor or a female missionary! You ought to know me better, Blanche.'

'I know you are fond of him,' the girl repeated resolutely. 'Why, you've changed your very nature for his sake! As if we didn't all of us know the influence that has made you take up Gertrude's work!'

Elizabeth burst out laughing.

'Perhaps I wanted to take the shine out of Gertrude's supernal virtues,' she said. 'Perhaps I wanted to show him that I was just as well able to do that kind of thing as his Hawleigh saints, who call it their vocation—that I was able to make the poor people love me, which very few of his saints can manage.'

'Upon my word, Lizzie, I'm afraid you're very wicked,' exclaimed Blanche, staring at her sister with an awed look.

Elizabeth was sitting on the edge of the low French bed, her brown hair falling round her like a sombre drapery, her eyes fixed with a dreamy look,

a half-mischievous, half-triumphant smile upon her
lips.

'I'm afraid you're right,' she said with a sudden
burst of candour. 'I feel intensely wicked at this
moment. Can you guess what I should like to do,
Blanche ?'

'Not I. You are the most unfathomable girl in
creation.'

'I should like to bring that man to my feet, to
make him as deeply in love with me as—as ever any
miserable slavish woman was with a man who did
not love her, and then spurn him ; fool him to the top
of his bent, Blanche ; and when I had become the
very apple of his eye—perhaps while he was deliberat-
ing in his slow dull soul as to whether he should
make an election between me and the conversion
of the South-Sea Islanders—astonish him some fine
morning by announcing my engagement with somebody a little better worth marrying. He would have
his South-Sea Islanders left to console him.'

She flung the cloud of hair back from her face
impatiently, with a bitter little laugh and a downward glance of the dark eyes, as if she did indeed
see Malcolm Forde at her feet, and were scorning
him.

Blanche gazed at her with unmitigated horror.

'Goodness gracious, Lizzie! What can put such dreadful ideas into your head? What has Malcolm Forde done to make you so savage?'

'What has he done? O, nothing, I suppose,' half hysterically. 'But I should like to punish him for all he has made me suffer to-day.'

CHAPTER VI.

When God smote His hands together, and struck out thy soul
as a spark
Into the organised glory of things, from deeps of the dark,— .
Say, didst thou shine, didst thou burn, didst thou honour the
power in the form,
As the star does at night, or the fire-fly, or even the little
ground worm?
'I have sinned,' she said,
'For my seed-light shed
Has smouldered away from His first decrees.
The cypress praiseth the fire-fly, the ground-leaf praiseth the
worm ;
I am viler than these.'

What had Malcolm Forde done ? The question
was one which that gentleman demanded of himself
not unfrequently during the next few weeks. Was it
wise or foolish to have bared his old wound before the
pitying, or unpitying, eyes of Elizabeth Luttrell; to
have made this appeal for womanly sympathy, he who
was by nature so reticent, who had kept his griefs so
sternly locked within his own breast until now ? Was
it wise or foolish ? Was he right in deeming her
nobler than the common herd of women, a soul with

whom it might be sweet to hold friendship's calm communion, a woman whom he dared cultivate as his friend? He was not even yet fully resolved upon this point; but of possible peril to himself in any such association he had never dreamed. Long ago he had told himself that his heart was buried in Alice Fraser's grave, laid at rest for ever in the hill-side burial-ground beneath the mountains that shelter Lanorgie; long ago he had solemnly devoted all the power of his intellect, all the vigour of his manhood, to the pursuit of a grander aim than that mere earthly happiness for which the majority of mankind searches. From that burial of all his human hopes there could be no such thing as resurrection. To be false to the memory of his lost bride, to forswear the oath he made to himself when he took his priestly vows, with a wider or a sterner view of the priestly office than is common to English churchmen—to do this would be to stamp himself for ever in his own esteem the weakest and meanest of mankind. Such a thing was simply impossible. He had therefore no snare to dread in friendly companionship with a bright generous-hearted young creature who was infinitely superior to her surroundings, a faulty soul vaguely struggling towards a purer atmosphere, a woman whom he might help to be good.

He felt that here was a noble nature in sore peril
of shipwreck, a creature with the grandest capabilities,
who might for lack of culture achieve nothing but evil;
a soul too easily led astray, a heart too impulsive to
resist temptation.

'If she were my sister, I would make her one of
the noblest women of her age,' he said to himself,
with a firm faith in his own influence upon this feebler
feminine spirit.

'Her very faults would seem charming to some
men,' he told himself sagely. 'That variableness
which makes her at times the most incomprehensible
of women, at other times the sweetest, would lead a
fool on to his destruction. There was a day when I
deemed her incapable of serious thought or unselfish
work; yet, once awakened to the sense of her obligations, there has been no limit to her patience and
devotion.'

And he was the author of this awakening. He
felt a natural pride and delight in the knowledge of
this. He was the Prometheus who had breathed the
higher and more spiritual life into the nostrils of this
lovely clay. He had snatched her from the narrow
influences of her home; from the easy-going thoughtless father, whose mind hardly soared above the consideration of his cellar or his dinner-table; from the

petty provincial society, with its petty gossip about
its own works and ways, the fashion of its garments,
and its dinings and tea-drinkings and trivial domestic
details, from Mrs. Smith's new parlour-maid to Mrs.
Brown's new bonnet. It was something to have lifted
her from this slough of despond even to the outer-
most edge of a better world.

Yet she had flashes of the old leaven, intervals of
retrogression that afflicted him sorely. During that
homeward drive from the picnic she had been all that
the most exacting of mankind could desire; sympathetic, confiding, understanding his every thought,
and eager to be understood; candid, unaffected,
womanly. But when the drive was over she had
changed, as quickly as Cinderella at midnight's first
fatal stroke. All the glorious vestments of her re-
generated soul had dropped away, leaving the old
familiar rags—the flippancy, the fastness, the inso-
lence of conscious beauty. That earnest talk by the
sundial, which Frederick Melvin had watched from
afar with jealous eyes, had been in reality expostula-
tion. The Curate had presumed to lecture his Vicar's
daughter, not in an insolent hectoring spirit, not in
a tone to which she could fairly object, but with a
gentle gravity, regretful that she who had so many
gifts should yet fall short of perfection.

' How can you talk such nonsense ?' she exclaimed
impetuously, with an angry movement of her graceful
shoulders. ' You know there is no one perfect, you
know there is no one good. Are you not always ham-
mering that at us in your sermons, making believe
to consider us the veriest dirt—yes, even Mrs. Pol-
whele, of the Dene, in her new French bonnet ? I
don't see any use in trying to please you. There
never was but one perfect woman, and she is
dead.'

' I do not think it very kind of you to speak like
that,' said Mr. Forde, ' as if you grudged my praise
of the dead.'

' No, it is not that ; but it seems hard that the
living should suffer because—because you choose to
brood upon the memory of some one who was better
than they. I will not shape myself by any model,
however perfect. Why,' with a little bitter laugh,
' if I were to become the faultless being you tell me
I might make myself, my perfection would only be a
plagiarism. I would rather be original, and keep my
sins. Besides, what can my shortcomings matter to
you ?'

' They matter very much to me. Do you think I
am interested in my congregation just for twenty
minutes, while I am preaching to them, and that

when I come down the pulpit-stairs all interest ceases till my next sermon ?'

'You should reserve your lectures for Gertrude. She enjoys sermonising and being sermonised. I believe she keeps a journal of her spiritual progress. I daresay she would like to show it to you. No doubt you would find plenty of my sins duly booked *en parenthèse.*'

'Your sister Gertrude is a very admirable person, and I was beginning to hope you would grow like her.'

'Thanks for the compliment. If I am in any danger of resembling Gertrude, I shall leave off trying to be good the first thing to-morrow morning.'

'Good-night, Miss Luttrell—'

'I am not Miss Luttrell. My name is Elizabeth.'

'Good-night, Elizabeth,' he said, very coldly; and before she could speak again he was gone, leaving her planted there by the sundial, angry with herself, and still more angry with him; passionately jealous of that memory which was more to him than the best and brightest of living creatures.

'Alice Fraser!' she said to herself. 'Alice Fraser! A Scotch clergyman's daughter, a girl who never had a well-made gown in her life, I daresay. It was her portrait I saw over the mantelpiece in his sitting-

room, no doubt. A poor little namby-pamby face,
with pleading eyes always seeming to say, " Forgive
me for being a little better than everybody else."
And that cup and saucer under the glass shade!
Hers, no doubt, used in her last illness. Poor girl!
it was hard to be stricken down like that; and yet
how sweet to die with his arms holding her, his
agonised face bent over hers, his quivering lips put
close to hers to catch the last faint breath! What
was there in that poor little meek-souled thing to
hold him in life, and after death—to set a seal upon
his strong heart, and keep it even in her grave? It
is more than I can understand.'

In the brief intervals of leisure which his daily
duties left him—very brief at the best—Mr. Forde
found his thoughts return with a strange persistency
to the image of Elizabeth Luttrell. It was not that
he saw her often, for they had not encountered each
other since the picnic, the young lady having been
absent when he paid his duty-call at the Vicarage. It
was perhaps because she was less agreeable than other
women; because she rebelled and defied him, and
argued with him flippantly, where other damsels
bowed down and worshipped; because she had never
weakened her optic nerves by a laborious course of

tent-stitch and satin-stitch; because she had refused
to lead the choir of Sunday-school children, or to
take a class in the Sunday-school; because she was
in every respect, save in her late amendment in the
district-visiting way, exactly what a clergyman's
daughter ought not to be, that Malcolm Forde suffered
his mind to dwell upon her in the dead watches of
the night, and gave her a very disproportionate
amount of his consideration at all times and seasons.

Of late he had been seriously disturbed about
her; for shortly after the picnic there came a change
in the damsel's conduct, a sad falling away in her
district-visiting. The women whom she had attached
to her bewailed this fact to Mr. Forde.

'I thought as how she'd been ill, poor dear,' said
one; 'but when I went to church last Sunday, there
she was, with her head held as high as ever, like a
queen, bless her handsome face, and more colour in
her cheeks than she used to have. She sent me a
gownd last week by the vicarage housemaid, and a
regular good one, not a brack in it; but though I
was humbly thankful, I'd rather have seen her, as I
used when she'd come and sit agen my wash-tub
reading the Gospel.'

He heard this lamentation, in different forms,
from several women, and after some inquiry discovered

that, except to visit a sick child, Elizabeth had not
been among her people since the day of the picnic at
Lawborough Beeches. She had sent them tea, and
small benefactions of that kind, by the hand of a
menial,—benefactions for which they were duly grateful,—but they missed her visits not the less.

'She's such good company,' remarked one woman; 'not like most of your districk-visitors, which
make you feel that down-hearted as if you'd had a
undertaker talkin' to you. She's got such pleasant
lively ways, and yet as pitiful as pitiful if there's sickness. And she do make herself so at home in one's
place. "Let me dust your chimbleypiece, Mrs.
Morris," she says to me; and dusts it before I can
look, and sets the things out so pretty, and brings
me that there blue chaney vaise next day, bless her
kind heart!'

Mr. Forde was deeply grieved by this falling off.
It seemed as if the Promethean spark had been untimely blown out. The beautiful clay was once more
only clay. He felt unspeakably disheartened by the
straying of this one lamb, which he had sought to
gather into the fold.

Once possessed of his facts, he went straightway
to the Vicarage to remonstrate.

'I do not care how obnoxious I render myself to

her,' he thought. 'I am not here to speak smooth words. If her father neglects his duty, there is so much more reason I should do mine.'

The year had grown six weeks older since the picnic. In summer time the Luttrell girls—with the exception of Gertrude, who was always busy—lived for the most part a straggling life, scattering themselves about garden and orchard, and doing all things in a desultory manner. In summer the Curate might have felt tolerably sure of finding Elizabeth alone under some favourite tree, reading a novel, or making believe to work. To-day it was different. The October afternoon was fine, but chill. He would have to seek his erring sister in the house, to inquire for the Vicar and the young ladies after the usual manner of visitors, and to take his chance of getting a few words alone with Elizabeth.

He looked right and left of the winding path as he went from the garden-gate to the house, but saw no glimpse of feminine apparel athwart the tall holly-hocks; so he was fain to go on to the hall-door. He was not particularly observant of details; but it struck him that the gray old house had a smarter aspect than usual. The carriage drive had been lately rolled; there was even some indication of a thin coating of new gravel. Muslin curtains that were unfamiliar to

his eyes shrouded the bow-windows of the drawing-
room, and a little yapping black-and-tan terrier—the
veriest abbreviation of the dog species—flew out of a
half-open door to gird at him as he rang the bell.

The vicarage parlour-maid—a young woman he
had prepared for confirmation twelve months before—
came smiling to admit him. Even she had an altered
air—more starch in her gown, a smart white apron,
cherry-coloured bows in her cap.

'Is Mr. Luttrell at home?'

'No, sir. Master went to Bulford in the pony-
chaise with Miss Luttrell directly after lunch. But
the other young ladies are in the drawing-room, sir,
and Mrs. Chevenix.'

He went into the hall—a square low-ceilinged
chamber, embellished with antiquated cabinets of
cracked oriental china; an ancient barometer; a pair
of antlers, with a fox's brush lying across them, both
trophies of the Vicar's prowess in the field; a smoky-
looking piece of still-life, with the usual cut lemon
and dead leveret and monster bunch of impossible
grapes; the still smokier portrait of an old gentleman
of the pigtail period; and sundry other specimens of
art, which, massed into one lot of oddments at an
auction, might possibly have realised a five-pound
note.

'Mrs. Chevenix?' said the Curate interroga-
tively.

'Yes, sir—the young ladies' aunt, sir—master's
sister.'

'O,' said Mr. Forde. He faintly remembered
having heard of this lady—the well-to-do aunt and
godmother who had given Diana the grand piano; an
aunt who was sometimes alluded to confidently by
Blanche as an authority upon all matters of taste and
fashion; a person possessed of a universal knowledge,
of the lighter sort; whose judgment as to the best
book or the cleverest picture of the season was a
judgment beyond dispute; who knew the ins and outs
of life aristocratic and life diplomatic, and would
naturally be one of the first persons to be informed
of an approaching marriage in fashionable circles or
an impending war.

Without ever having seen this lady, Mr. Forde
had, from his inner consciousness, as it were, evolved
some faint image of her, and the image was eminently
distasteful to him. He disliked Mrs. Chevenix, more
or less on the Dr. Fell principle. The reason why
he could not tell, but he most assuredly did dislike
her.

He could understand now that the new muslin
curtains and the sprinkling of new gravel were ex-

penses incurred in honour of this superior person.
He kept his hat in his hand,—he would have left it
in the hall, most likely, had the young ladies been
alone,—and thus armed, went in to be presented to
Mrs. Chevenix.

'O, how do you do, Mr. Forde?' cried Diana,
bouncing up from the hearthrug, where she had been
caressing the infinitesimal terrier. 'You are quite a
stranger. We never see you now, except in church.
Let me present you to my aunt, Mrs. Chevenix.'

He had a sense of something large and brown and
rustling rising with a stately air between him and
the light, and then slowly sinking into the luxurious
depths of a capacious arm-chair; a chair not in-
digenous to the vicarage drawing-room, evidently an
additional luxury provided for aunt Chevenix.

He had shaken hands with Diana, and bowed to
aunt Chevenix—who maintained an aristocratic reserve on the subject of hand-shaking, and did not go
about the world offering her hand to the first comer—
in a somewhat absent-minded manner. He had performed these two ceremonies with his eyes wandering
in quest of that other Miss Luttrell for whose special
behalf he had come to the Vicarage.

She—Elizabeth—sat in a low chair by the fire,
reading a novel, the very picture of contented idle-

ness. She too, like the house, seemed to him altered. Her garments had a more fashionable air. That puritan simplicity she had assumed at the beginning of her career as a district-visitor was entirely discarded. She wore lockets and trinkets which he had not seen her wear of late, and rich plaits of dark-brown hair were piled high on the graceful head, like the pictures in fashion-books.

She rose now to greet him with a languid air, an elegant indifference of manner which he surmised had been imparted by the stately personage in lustrous brown silk. They shook hands coldly enough on both sides, and Elizabeth resumed her seat, with her book open in her lap.

Mrs. Chevenix sat with her portly brown-silk back towards the bow-window. It was one of Mrs. Chevenix's principles to sit with her back to the light, whereby a *soupçon* of pearl-powder and hair-dye was rendered less obvious to the observer. A beauty had Mrs. Chevenix been in her time, ay, and as acknowledged a beauty as Elizabeth Luttrell herself, although it would have cost Malcolm Forde a profound effort of faith to believe that vivid flashing brunette loveliness of Elizabeth's could ever develop into the fleshly charms of the matron. But in certain circles, and in her own estimation, Mrs. Chevenix still

took high rank as a fine woman. She had arrived at
that arid full-blown stage of existence in which a
woman can only be distinguished as fine, in which a
carefully preserved figure and a complexion eked out
by art are the last melancholy vestiges of departed
beauty.

She was a large person, with a large aquiline-
nosed countenance framed by broad-plaited bands of
flaxen hair. Her cheeks bloomed with the florid
bloom of middle age, delicately toned down by a
judicious application of pearl-powder; her arched
eyebrows were several shades darker than her hair,
and a little too regular for nature; her eyes were
blue—cold calculating eyes, which looked as if they
had never beheld the outer world as anything better
than a theatre for the advancement and gratification
of self; or at least this was the idea which those
chilly azure orbs inspired in the mind of Mr. Forde
as he sat opposite the lady, talking small talk and
telling Diana Luttrell the news of his parish.

Mrs. Chevenix had a certain good-society manner
which was as artificial as her eyebrows, or the bluish-
white tints that toned her cheek-bones; and of this
manner she kept two samples always in stock—the
gushing and vivacious style which she affected with
people whom she deemed her superiors, the listless

and patronising, or secondary manner, wherewith she gratified her inferiors.

It was of course not likely she would take the trouble to gush for her brother's curate, even though he might be a person of decent family, and possessed of independent means. Had he been an 'Honourable,' a scion, however remote, of some distinguished house in the peerage, she would have beamed upon him with her most entrancing smiles. But an unknown Scotchman; a man who had been described to her as terribly in earnest; a person of revolutionary principles, who set himself against the existing order of things, wanting to reform this and that, and perhaps to level the convenient barriers which keep the common herd in their proper places; a dismal person, no doubt, full of strange wailings, like the ancient prophets, whom she heard wonderingly sometimes at church, giving them just as much attention as she could spare from the fair vista of new bonnets shining in a shaft of light from the gothic window, and who seemed to her to have been distracted personages eminently ineligible for dinner-parties.

'Aunt Chevenix missed your sermon last Sunday morning, Mr. Forde,' said Diana. 'She had one of her headaches, and was afraid the church might be hot.'

'In October?' said Mr. Forde, smiling. 'Our congregation is not vast enough for that.' He did not express any regret about his loss of such a hearer as aunt Chevenix.

'I am really fond of a good sermon,' remarked the lady blandly, trifling with a shining black fan, wherewith she was wont to flap the empty air at all times and seasons. This fan, a gold-rimmed eye-glass, and a double-headed scent-bottle, were Mrs. Chevenix's only means of employment, after she had read the *Morning Post* and accomplished her diurnal tale of letter-writing. 'And good sermons are become so rare,' she went on in her slow pompous way. 'I have heard no eloquent preacher for the last five years, except the Bishop of Granchester.'

'You would not say that if you had heard Mr. Forde,' said Diana.

Mrs. Chevenix put up her eyeglass and looked at the Curate with a languid smile, as if with the aid of that instrument she were able to make a precise estimate of his powers.

'Mr. Forde is a young man, my dear. It is hardly fair to name him in the same breath with the bishop.'

Elizabeth, who had been turning the leaves of her book listlessly with an air of absolute inattention, flashed out at this.

'Mr. Forde is natural,' she said, 'which is more than I can say for the bishop. I admit his eloquence, his grand bass voice, sinking to an almost awful solemnity at every climax. But it seems to me a tutored eloquence. I could fancy him an actor in a Greek play, declaiming behind a mask. Mr. Forde' —a sudden pause, as if she had been going to say a great deal, and had hastily checked herself—'is different.'

Malcolm Forde listened with eyes bent on the ground; but just at the last words, he raised those dark deep-set eyes, and glanced at the speaker. What a splendid face it was, with its look of intense life, its scorn of scorn, or love of love ; a nature in all things intensified, like that typical poet who in a golden clime was born.

'Yes, she *is* a noble creature,' he said to himself. 'No matter how capricious, or fickle, or unstable. She is a creature of fire and light, and she shall not be lost, not for all the aunt Chevenixes in the world.'

He cast a swift glance of defiance at the harmless matron in brown silk and flaxen plaits crowned with blonde and artificial roses, as if she had been the foul fiend himself, and he playing a desperate game of chess with her for this fair young soul. He had always disliked the family fetish, when she had been

only a remote and unknown image to be invoked ever
when there was question of the proprieties.   But he
disliked her most of all now, when she was seated
within the citadel, and was poisoning the atmosphere
of Elizabeth's home with her worldly spirit.

He was swift to condemn and to suspect, perhaps,
since he had seen very little of the lady as yet ; but
that inane small-talk, that stale gossip of Eaton-
square and Lancaster-gate, that bismuth-shaded
cheek, that practicable eyebrow, which elevated itself
with a trained expression of irony, or drooped with a
studied languor—all these artificialities told him the
nature of the woman, and told him that she was the
last of creatures whom he would care to see in daily
communion with a girl whose wayward disposition
had of late been curiously interesting to him.

That dogmatic assertion of his superiority even to
a bishop, hurled at the very teeth of the family idol,
pleased him mightily.   It was not conceit that was
gratified—it was sweet to him to discover that, in
spite of all her affected scorn, this girl appreciated
him.

He did not acknowledge her compliment, except
by one brief smile—that slow quiet curve of the firm
thoughtful lips, which was sweeter than common
smiles.   He went on patiently with the morning-

caller talk, listened tolerantly to small scraps of information about the Lancaster-gateites, until he could fairly rise to depart. But he did not mean to leave the Vicarage with his mission unfulfilled.

'Will you give me a few minutes in the garden?' he said in a low voice, as he shook hands with Elizabeth. 'I want to talk to you about your cottagers.'

The ears of the Chevenix, more acute than those chilly blue eyes which required the aid of binoculars, pricked up at this sound of confidential converse.

'Did I hear you say something about cottagers, Mr. Forde?' she demanded sharply.

'Yes,' he replied; 'I was speaking of that order of creatures.' He was strongly tempted to add, 'who do not inhabit Lancaster-gate,' but judiciously held his peace.

'Then I must beg that you do not put any more nonsense about district-visiting into my niece's head. It is all very well for Gertrude, who is strong, physically and mentally, and is not of so impressionable a nature as Elizabeth, and is some years older, into the bargain. I consider there is more than enough done for the poor in this place. My brother gives away half his income, and spends as much of his time amongst his parishioners as—as—his health will permit. Besides which he has of course a powerful

auxiliary in his curate, whose duty it is, naturally, to
devote himself to that kind of thing. And then there
are always maiden ladies in a place—good-hearted
dowdy souls, who delight in that sort of work; so
that you can hardly be in want in aid. But, however that may be, I cannot possibly allow my niece to
fatigue herself and excite herself as she has done at
your suggestion. I found her in a really low state
when I came here—depressed in spirits, and nervous
to the last degree.'

Elizabeth flamed crimson at this.

'How can you talk such nonsense, aunt?' she
cried angrily, being the only one of the sisters who
was not habitually overawed by aunt Chevenix. 'I
am sure I was well enough; but those London doctors put such twaddle into your head.'

Mrs. Chevenix sighed gently, and gravely shook
the head which was accused of harbouring professional
twaddle.

'If your niece is to go to heaven, I fancy she will
have to travel by her own line of country, without reference to you, Mrs. Chevenix,' said Malcolm Forde.
'I do not think she will submit to be forbidden to do
her duty among her father's flock. It is not a question of just what is most conducive to health or high
spirits. I do not say that I would have *her*'—this

with an almost tender emphasis on the pronoun—
' sacrifice health or length of years even for the holi-
est work, but we know such sacrifices are only the
natural expression of a perfect faith. I am not asking her to do anything hard or unpleasant, however.
For her, the yoke may be of the easiest, the burden
of the lightest. If you knew, as I do, how in two or
three months she has contrived to win the hearts of
these people—what good her influence may do almost
unconsciously on her part—I think you would hardly
talk about forbidding her to give some time and
thought to her father's poor.'

He spoke warmly, and it was the first time that
anything approaching praise had dropped from his
lips. Elizabeth looked at him with a glowing face,
dark eyes that brightened as they looked.

' Thank you, Mr. Forde,' she said; 'I did not
know I was of any use, and I got disheartened; and
when aunt Chevenix came, I gave the business up
altogether. But I shall begin again to-morrow.'

Aunt Chevenix stared at Elizabeth, and from
Elizabeth to Mr. Forde, with the stony stare of
speechless indignation.

' O, very well, my dear,' she said to her niece at
last. ' Of course, you must know best what is conducive to your own happiness.' And then she sniffed

a sniff, as who should say, ' I can bequeath my money elsewhere.   You have sisters, my foolish Elizabeth, as dependent as yourself.   I can instruct my solicitor to prepare a codicil revoking that clause in my will which has reference to your interests.'

Mr. Forde had gained his point, and cared very little what smothered fires might be glowing in the Chevenix breast.   Elizabeth went out into the garden with him, bare-headed, heedless of a chill October nor'-wester, and heard all he could tell her about her neglected poor, questioning him eagerly.

' Poor souls, are they really fond of me ?' she exclaimed remorsefully.   ' I did not know it was in me to do any good.'

On this Malcolm Forde grew eloquent, told her as he had never told her before the value of such a soul as hers, gifted with rare capabilities, with powers so far above life's ordinary level; urged her to rise superior to her surroundings, to be something greater and better than the common new-bonnet-worshipping young-ladyhood of Hawleigh.

' I am not depreciating your home or your family, Elizabeth,' he said, remembering that she had accorded him this free use of her Christian name ; ' but the world has grown so worldly, even religion seems to have lost its spirituality.   There is a trading spirit, an assumption of fashion, in our very temples. Indeed, I am sometimes doubtful whether our floral decorations and embroidered altar-cloths are not a delusion and a snare. It should be good to make our churches beautiful; yet there are moments when I doubt the wisdom of these things. They make too direct an appeal to the senses. I find myself yearning for the stern simplicity of the Scottish Church—that unembellished service which Edward Irving could make so vast an instrument for the regeneration of mankind. He had no flower-decked chancel, no white-robed choir. It was only a voice crying in the city-wilderness.'

This he said meditatively, straying from the chief subject of his discourse, and giving expression almost involuntarily to a doubt that had been tormenting him of late. He brought himself back to the more personal question of Elizabeth's spiritual welfare presently.

'Why did you keep away from your people?' he asked. 'Were you really ill? or was it your aunt's influence?'

She looked at him with a mischievous daring in her eyes.

'Neither one nor the other.'

'Then why was it? You had been going on so

well and so steadily, and I was beginning to be proud
of you. I trust—' this slowly, and with hesitation—
'I trust there was nothing I said that day at the picnic which could have a deterring influence, or which
could have offended you.'

'I was not offended,' she answered, her lips
quivering faintly, her face turned away from him.
'What was there to offend me? Only you made me
feel myself so poor a creature, my highest efforts so
infinitely beneath your ideal of perfect womanhood, my
feeble struggles at self-improvement so mean and
futile measured by your heroic standard, that I did
perhaps feel a little discouraged, a little inclined to
give up striving to make myself what nature had
evidently not intended me to be—an estimable
woman.'

'Nature intended you to be good and great,'
answered Mr. Forde earnestly.

'But not like Alice Fraser,' said Elizabeth, with
a bitter smile.

'There are different kinds of perfection. Hers
was an innate and unconscious purity, a limitless
power of self-sacrifice. She was the ideal daughter
of the manse, a creature who had never known a
selfish thought, to whom the labours which I press
upon you as a duty were a second nature. She had

never lived except for others. I cannot say less or more of her than I told you that day—she was simply perfect. Yet you have gifts which she did not possess—a more energetic nature, a quicker intelligence. There is no good or noble work a woman can do in this world that you could not do, if you chose.'

Elizabeth shook her head doubtfully.

'I have no endurance,' she said; 'I am vain and feeble. O, believe me, I have by no means a lofty estimate of my own character. I require to be sustained by constant praise. It is all very well while you are encouraging me, I feel capable of anything; but when I have gone plodding on for two or three months longer, and you take my good conduct for granted, I shall grow weary again, and fall away again.'

'Not if you will look to a higher source for support and inspiration. My praises are a very poor reward. Trust to the approval of your own conscience rather; and forgive me if I urge you to keep yourself free from the influence of Mrs. Chevenix. It seems impertinent in me, no doubt, to presume to judge a lady I have only seen for half an hour—'

'O, pray don't apologise,' exclaimed Elizabeth in her careless way; 'I have a perfect appreciation of aunt Chevenix. She is the family idol; the goddess whom we all worship, conciliating her with all manner of sacrifices of our 'own inclinations. She presides over us in spirit even when at a distance, imparting her oracles in letters. Of course she is the very essence of worldliness. Is it not written in all the roses that garnish her cap? But she married a clever barrister, who blossomed in due course into a county-court judge, and died five years ago of a fit of apoplexy, which was considered the natural result of a prolonged series of dinners, leaving aunt Chevenix fifteen hundred a year at her own disposal. She never had any children, and we four girls are all she can boast of in the way of nephews or nieces, so it is an understood thing the fifteen hundred a year must ultimately come to us, and we are paying aunt Chevenix in advance for her bounty, by deferring to her in all things. She is not half so bad as you might suppose from her little pompous ways and her fan and eye-glass ; and I really think she is fond of us.'

Not a pleasing confession to a man of Malcolm Forde's temperament from the lips of a beautiful girl. This waiting for dead men's shoes was of all modern vices the one that seemed to him meanest.

'I hope you will not allow your conduct to be influenced by any consideration of your reversionary interest in Mrs. Chevenix's income,' he said gravely.

'You need have no fear of that,' she answered lightly. 'I never took any one's advice in my life—except perhaps yours—and as to being dictated to by aunt Chevenix, that is quite out of the question. I am the only one of the family who defies her; and, strange to say, I enjoy the reputation of being her favourite.'

'I don't wish you to defy her,' said Mr. Forde, with his serious smile. She seemed to him at some moments only a wayward child, this girl whom he was urging to become good and great. 'You may be all that a niece should be—kind, affectionate, and respectful—and yet retain your right of judgment.'

He looked at his watch. He had been at the Vicarage more than an hour, and half that time had been spent walking to and fro beside the autumnal china-asters and chrysanthemums, with Elizabeth for his companion.

'I have detained you longer than I intended,' he said. 'I shall tell Mrs. Morris and Mrs. Brown that you are coming to see them. Good-bye.'

He stood by the broad barred gate—a homely farmhouse-looking gate, painted white—a tall vigorous figure, unclerical of aspect, with the erect soldierly air that had not departed from him on his change of profession, a man who looked like a leader of men, the dark earnest eyes looking downward at Elizabeth, the broad strong hand clasping hers with the firm clasp of friendship. Verily a tower of strength such a friend as this, worth a legion of the common clay which men and women count as friends.

Elizabeth stood by the gate watching him as he walked along the white high-road towards Hawleigh.

'He looks like a red-cross knight disguised in modern costume,' she said to herself; 'he looks like Hercules in a frock-coat. How different from slim little Mr. Adderley, picking his steps upon the dusty causeway. And now he will go from house to house, and teach, and read, and exhort, and help, and counsel, till ten o'clock to-night, with only just time for a hasty dinner between his labours. And yet he is never weary, and never thinks his life barren, and never longs to be in London among happy crowds of refined men and women enjoying all the delights that the science of pleasure can devise for them— operas, and concerts, and races, and picture-shows, and flower-shows, and a hundred gatherings together of taste, and beauty, and refinement. Does he ever long for that kind of life, I wonder, the very fringe or outer edge of which is delightful, if one may believe aunt Chevenix? Or does he languish for a roving life—as I do sometimes—among fair strange

countries, sailing on the blue waters of the Adriatic
or the Archipelago, among the sunny islands of the
old Greek world, or wandering in the shady depths
of the Black Forest, or on thymy mountain tops, or
amidst regions of everlasting snow? Has he no
hours of vain despondency and longing, as I have?
Or did he concentrate all his hopes and desires upon
Alice Fraser, and bury them all in her grave?'

She was in no hurry to return to the drawing-room
fireside and the Chevenix atmosphere of genteel idleness. Instead of going back to the house, she went
from the garden to the orchard, and paced that
grassy slope alone, circulating slowly among the
mossgrown trunks of the apple and cherry trees,
thinking of Malcolm Forde.

'How good he is,' she said to herself; 'how
earnest, how real! What a king among men! And
yet what hope is there for him in life? what prospect
of escape from this dull drudgery, which he must
surely sicken of, sooner or later? He has no interest
that can advance him in the Church—I have heard
him say that—so his preferment will most likely be
of the slowest. I hardly wonder that he sometimes
thinks of turning missionary. Better to be something—to win some kind of name in the centre of
Africa, or among the South-Sea Islands—than to be

buried alive in such a place as Hawleigh. And if he ever were to change his mind and marry, what a brilliant career for his wife!' She laughed bitterly at the thought. 'How I pity that poor demented soul, whoever she may be! And yet he seems to consider this kind of life perfect, and that one might be good and great; goodness and greatness consisting in perpetual district-visiting, unlimited plain needlework for the Dorcas Society, unfailing attendance at early services—all the dull, dull routine of a Christian life. Of the two careers, I should certainly prefer Africa!'

Thus did she argue with herself, this rebellious soul, who could not understand that life was intended to afford her anything but pleasure, the kind of pleasure her earthly nature pined for—operas, and concerts, and horses and carriages, and foreign travel. She roamed the orchard for nearly an hour, meditating upon Malcolm Forde, his character, his aspirations, his prospects, and that hypothetical foolish woman who might be rash enough to accept him for her husband; and then went back to the drawing-room, to be sharply interrogated by aunt Chevenix.

'My dear Elizabeth, what a dishevelled creature you have made yourself!' exclaimed that lady, looking with disfavour at Lizzie's loosened hair and disordered neck ribbon. The young ladies of Eaton-place rarely exposed themselves to the wind, except at Brighton in November, when a certain license might be permitted.

'I have been walking in the orchard, aunt. It's rather blowy on that side of the house.'

'I hope you have not had that Mr. Forde with you all this time.'

'Mr. Forde has been gone nearly an hour. I wish you wouldn't call him *that* Mr. Forde. You may not mean anything by it, but it sounds unpleasant.'

'But I do mean something by it,' replied aunt Chevenix, fanning herself more vehemently than usual. 'I mean that your Mr. Forde is a most arrogant, disagreeable, under-bred person. To presume to dictate to my niece—to over-ride my authority before my very face! The man is evidently utterly unaccustomed to good society.'

'You might have said that of St. Peter or St. Paul, aunt,' replied Elizabeth in her coolest manner; 'neither of those belonged to the Eaton-place section of society. But Mr. Forde is a man of good family, and was in a crack cavalry regiment before he entered the Church. So you are out in your reckoning.'

'A crack regiment!' echoed the matron. 'Elizabeth, you have acquired a most horrible mode of

expression. Perhaps you have learnt that from Mr.
Forde, as well as a new version of your duty to your
relations. If ever that man was in a cavalry regiment, I should think it must have been in the
capacity of rough-rider. What a man-mountain the
creature is, too! I should hardly have thought any
sane bishop would have ordained such a giant.
There ought really to be a standard height for the
Church as well as for the army, excluding pigmies
and giants. I never beheld a man so opposite to
one's ideal of a curate.'

'O, of course,' cried Elizabeth impatiently.
'Your ideal curate is a slim simpering thing with
white hands—a bandboxical being, talking solemn
small-talk like a fashionable doctor—a kettledrumish-
man, always dropping in at afternoon tea. We
have had three of that species, varying only in detail.
Thank heaven, Malcolm Forde is something better
than that.'

'I cannot perceive that you have any occasion to
feel grateful to Providence upon the subject of Mr.
Forde's character and attributes, let them be what
they may,' said Mrs. Chevenix; 'and I consider that
familiar mention of your father's curate—a paid servant, remember, like a governess or a cook—to the
last degree indecorous.'

'But I do thank heaven for him,' cried Elizabeth recklessly. 'He is my friend and counsellor,—the only man I ever looked up to—'

'You appear to forget that you have a father,' murmured Mrs. Chevenix, sitting like a statue, with her closed fan laid across her breast, in a stand-at-ease manner.

'I don't forget anything of the kind; but I never looked up to *him*. It isn't in human nature to reverence one's father. One is behind the scenes of his life, you see. One knows all his little impatiences, his unspiritual views on the subject of dinner, his intolerance of crumpled roseleaves in his domestic arrangements. Papa is a dear old thing, but he is of the earth, earthy. Mr. Forde is of another quality,—spiritual, earnest, self-sacrificing, somewhat arbitrary, perhaps, in the consciousness of his own strength, but gentle even when he commands; capable of a heroic life which my poor feeble brain cannot even imagine; his eager spirit even now yearning to carry God's truth to some wretched people buried in creation's primeval gloom; ready to die a martyr in some nameless isle of the Pacific, in some unknown desert in Central Africa. He is my modern St. Paul, and I reverence him.'

Elizabeth indulged herself with this small tirade

half in earnest, half in a mocking spirit, amusing herself with the discomfiture of aunt Chevenix, who sat
staring at her in speechless horror.

'The girl is stark mad!' gasped the matron,
with a faint flutter of her fan, slowly recovering
speech and motion.   'Has this sort of thing been
going on long, Diana?'

'Well, not quite so bad as this,' replied Diana;
'but I don't think Lizzie has been quite herself since
she took up the district-visiting.   She has left off
wearing nice gloves, and dressing for dinner, and
behaving in a general way like a Christian.'

'Has she, indeed?' said aunt Chevenix; 'then
the district-visiting must be put a stop to at once
and for ever, or it will leave her stranded high and
dry on the barren shore of old-maidism.   You may
be a very pretty girl, Elizabeth Luttrell—I daresay
you know you are tolerably good-looking, so there's no
use in my pretending you are not—but if once you
take up ultra-religious views, visiting the poor, and
all that kind of thing, I wash my hands of you.   I
had hoped to see you make a brilliant marriage; indeed, I have heard you talk somewhat over-confidently
of your carriage, your opera-box, your town house and
country seat.   But from what I hear to-day, I con-
clude your highest ambition is to marry this prepos-

terous curate—who looks a great deal more like a brigand chief, by the way—and devote your future existence to Sunday-school teaching and tea-meetings.'

Elizabeth stood tall and straight before her accuser, with clasped hands resting on the back of a prie-dieu chair, exactly as she had stood while she delivered her small rhapsody about Mr. Forde, stately and spiritual-looking as Joan of Arc inspired by her ' voices.'

'Perhaps, after all, it might be a woman's loftiest ambition to mate with Malcolm Forde,' she said slowly, with a tender dreamy look in her eyes; and then, before the dragon could remonstrate, she went on with a sudden change of manner, 'Don't be alarmed, auntie; I'm not going to hold the world well lost for love. I mean to have my opera-box, if it ever comes begging this way, and to give great dinners, with cabinet ministers and foreign ambassadors for my guests, and to be mistress of a country seat or two, and do wonderful things at elections, and to be stared at at country race-meetings, and to tread in that exalted path in which you would desire to train my ignorant footstep.

Mrs. Chevenix gave a half-despairing sigh.

'You are a most incomprehensible girl,' she said, 'and give me more trouble of mind than your three sisters put together. But I do hope that you will keep clear of any entanglement with that tall curate, a dangerous man, I am convinced; any flirtation of that kind would inevitably compromise you in the future. As to cabinet dinners and country seats, such marriages as you talk of are extremely rare nowadays, and for a Devonshire parson's daughter to make such a match would be a kind of miracle. But with your advantages you ought certainly to marry well; and it is better to look too high than too low. A season in London might do wonders.'

This London season was the shining bait which Mrs. Chevenix was wont to dangle before the eyes of her nieces, and by virtue of which she obtained their submission to her amiable caprices when the more remote advantage of inheritance might have failed to influence them. Gertrude and Diana had enjoyed each her season, and had not profited thereby in any substantial manner. They had been 'much admired,' Mrs. Chevenix declared with an approving air, especially Diana, as the livelier of the two; but admiration had not taken that definite form for which the soul of the match-maker longeth.

'There must be something wanting,' Mrs. Chevenix said pensively, in moments of confidence. 'I
find that something wanting in most of the girls of
the present day. Alfred Chevenix proposed to me in
my first season. I was a thoughtless thing just
emerged from the nursery, and his was not my only
offer. But my nieces made a very different effect.
Young men were attentive to them—Sir Harold Haw-
buck even seemed struck with Diana—but nothing
came of it. There must be a deficiency in something. Gertrude is too serious, Diana a shade too
flippant. It is manner, my dear, manner, in which
the rising generation is wanting.'

'A season in town,' cried Elizabeth, her dark eyes
sparkling, her head lifted with a superb arrogance,
and all thought of Malcolm Forde and the life spiritual for the moment banished. 'Yes, it is my turn,
is it not, auntie? and I think it is time I came out.
Who knows how soon I may begin to lose whatever
good looks I now possess? I am of a nervous temper; impressionable, as you suggested just now. I
have a nack of sleeping badly when my mind is full
of a subject, and excitement of any kind spoils my
appetite. Even the idea of a new bonnet will keep
me awake. I lie tossing from side to side all night
trying to determine whether it shall be pink or blue.

Living at this rate, I may be a positive fright before I am twenty; no complexion can stand against such wear and tear.'

'You have been allowed to grow up with a sadly undisciplined mind, my poor child,' Mrs. Chevenix said sententiously. 'If your papa had engaged a competent governess, a person who had lived in superior families, and was experienced in the training of the human mind and the figure—your waist measures two inches more than it ought at your age—his daughters would have done him much greater credit. But it was only like my brother Wilmot to grudge the expenditure of sixty guineas a year for a proper instructress of his daughters, while frittering away hundreds on his pauper parishioners.'

'Now, that is one of the things for which I *do* reverence papa,' cried Elizabeth with energy. 'Thank heaven, neither our minds nor our bodies have been trained by a professional trainer. Imagine growing like a fruit-tree nailed against a wall; every spontaneous outshoot of one's character cut back, every impulse pruned away as a non-fruit-bearing branch! I do bless papa with all my free untutored soul for having spared us that. But don't let us quarrel about details, dear auntie. Give me my season in London, and see what I will do. I languish for my opera-box and barouche, and the kind of life one reads of in Mrs. Gore's novels.'

'You shall spend next May and June with me,' said Mrs. Chevenix with another plaintive sigh. 'It will be hard work going over all the same ground again which I went over for Gerty and Di, but the result may be more brilliant.'

'Couldn't you manage to turn me off at the same time, auntie?' demanded Blanche pertly.

'I am sorry Gertrude and I were not fortunate enough to receive proposals from dukes or merchant princes,' said Diana, whose aristocratic features had flushed angrily at her aunt's implied complaint. 'Perhaps we might have been luckier if we had met more people of that kind. But of course Lizzie will do wonders. She reminds me of Mirabeau's remark about Robespierre; she will do great things, because she believes in herself.'

Elizabeth was prompt to respond to this attack; and so, with small sisterly bickerings, the conversation ended.

CHAPTER VII.

'Je ne voudrais pas, si j'étais Julie,
        N'être que jolie
        Avec ma beauté.
Jusqu'au bout des doigts je serais duchesse.
        Comme ma richesse
        J'aurais ma fierté.'

ELIZABETH, having in a manner pledged herself to a
career of worldly-mindedness, to begin in the ensuing
spring, deemed herself at liberty to follow her own
inclinations in the interim, and these inclinations
pointed to the kind of life which Malcolm Forde
wished her to lead.   She went back to her district-
work on the morning after the Curate's visit; put on
her Puritan hat and sober gray carmelite gown, which
seemed to her mind the whole armour of righteous-
ness, and went back to her people.   She was welcomed
back with an affection that at once surprised and
touched her.   She had done so little for them—only
treating them and thinking of them as creatures of
the same nature as herself—and yet they were so
grateful, and so fond of her.

So Elizabeth went back to what Gertrude called

her 'duties,' and the soul of aunt Chevenix was heavy
within her.   That lady had cherished high hopes
upon the subject of this lovely niece of hers.   A perfect beauty in a family is a fortune in embryo.   There
was no knowing what transcendent heights upon the
vast mountain range of 'good society' such a girl as
Elizabeth might scale, dragging her kith and kin up-
wards with her; provided she were but plastic in the
hands of good advisers.   To scheme, to plan, to
diplomatise, were natural operations of the Chevenix
mind.   A childless widow, with a comfortable income and a somewhat extended circle of acquaintance,
could hardly spend all her existence with no more
mental pabulum than a fan and a scent-bottle, and
the trivial amenities of polite life.   Mrs. Chevenix's
intellect must have lapsed into stagnation but for the
agreeable employment afforded by social diplomacy.
She knew everything about everybody; kept a mental
ledger in which she registered all the little weaknesses of her acquaintance; and had even a journal
wherein a good deal of genteel scandal was booked in
pen and ink.   But although by no means essentially
good-natured, she was not a mischief-maker, and no
unfriendly criticism or lady-like scandal had ever been
brought home to her.   She was, on the other hand,
renowned as a peace-maker: and if she had a fault,

it was a species of amiable officiousness, which some
of her acquaintance were inclined inwardly to resent.
Malign tongues had called Mrs. Chevenix a busy-
body; but in the general opinion she was a lady of
vivacious and agreeable manners, who gave snug little dinners, and elegant little suppers after concerts
and operas; and was a fine figure for garden-parties,
or a spare seat at the dinner-table; a lady who had
done some good service in the way of match-making,
and who exercised considerable influence over the
minds of divers young matrons whom she had assisted in the achievement of their matrimonial successes.

It seemed a hard thing that, after having been so
useful an ally to various damsels who were only the
protégées of the hour, Mrs. Chevenix's diplomatic
efforts in relation to her own nieces should result in
utter failure. She had never hoped very much from
Gertrude, who had that air of being too good for this
world, which is of all things the most repellent to
sinful man. Still, even for Gertrude Mrs. Chevenix
had done her best, bravely, and with the sublime
patience engendered by profound experience of this
mundane sphere, its difficulties and disappointments.
She had exhibited her seriously-minded niece at
charity bazaars, at déjeûners given after the inaugu-

ration of church organs, at choir festivals, and even
—with a noble sacrifice of personal inclination—at
Sunday-school tea-drinkings, orphanage fêtes, and
other assemblages of what this worldly-minded matron called the goody-goody school. She had angled
for popular preachers, for rectors and vicars, the value
of whose benefices she had looked up in the Clergy-
list; but she had cast her lines in vain. The popular preachers, crying from their pulpits that all is
vanity, were yet caught, moth-like, by the flame of
worldly beauties, and left Gertrude to console herself
with the calm contemplation of her own virtues, and
the conviction that they were somewhat too lofty for
the appreciation of vulgar clay. It had happened
thus, that with the advent of Malcolm Forde, the
eldest Miss Luttrell fancied she had at last met the
elect and privileged individual predestined to sympathise with, and understand her; the man upon whose
broad forehead she at once recognised the apostolic
grace, and who, she fondly hoped, would hail in her
the typical maiden of the church primitive and unde-
filed, the Dorcas or Lydia of modern civilisation. It
had been a somewhat bitter disappointment, therefore,
to discover that Mr. Forde, although prompt with the
bestowal of his confidence and friendship, was very
slow to exhibit any token of a warmer regard. Surely

he, so different in every attribute from all former curates, was not going to resemble them in their foolish worship at the shrine of Elizabeth. So long as this damsel had stuck to her accustomed line of worldliness, Gertrude had scarcely trembled. But when her younger sister all of a sudden subdued her somewhat reckless spirit, and took to district-visiting, Miss Luttrell's heart sank within her. She had no belief in the reality of this conversion. It was a glaring and bold-faced attempt at the Curate's subjugation, to bend that stiff neck beneath the yoke which had been worn so patiently by the flute-playing, verse-quoting Levites of the past. And Gertrude did not hesitate to express herself in somewhat bitter phrases to that effect.

When Diana came to Eaton-place for the season, the hopes of aunt Chevenix rose higher. The second Miss Luttrell was decidedly handsome, in the aquiline-nosed style, and was as decidedly stylish; wore her country-made gowns with an air which made them pass for the handicraft of a West-end mantua-maker; dressed her own hair with a skill which would have done credit to an experienced lady's-maid; and seemed altogether an advantageous young person for whom to labour. Yet Diana's season, though brightened by many a hopeful ray, had been barren of results. Perhaps these girls in their aunt's house were too obviously ' on view.' Mrs. Chevenix's renown as a match-maker may have gone against them; her past successes may have induced this present failure. And if Gertrude erred on the side of piety, Diana possibly went a thought too far in the matter of worldliness. She was clever and imitative, and caught-up the manners of more experienced damsels with a readiness that was perhaps too ready. She had perhaps a trifle too much confidence in herself; too much of the *veni, vidi, vici* style; went into battle with ' An opera-box and a house in Hyde-park-gardens' blazoned on her banner; and after suffering the fitful fever of high hopes that alternate with blank despair, Diana was fain to go back to Hawleigh Vicarage without being able to boast of any definite offer.

But with Elizabeth, Mrs. Chevenix told herself, things would be utterly different. She possessed that rare beauty which always commands attention. She was as perfect in her line as those heaven-born winners of Derby, Oaks, and Leger, which, by their performances as two-year-olds, proclaim themselves at once the conquerors of the coming year. Fairly good-looking girls were abundant enough every season, just as fairly good horses abound at every sale of yearlings throughout the sporting year; but there was as much difference between Elizabeth Luttrell and the common herd of pretty girls—all more or less dependent on the style of their bonnets, or the dressing of their hair for their good looks—as between the fifty-guinea colt, whose good points excite vague hopes of future merit in the breast of the speculative buyer, and a lordling of a crack stable, with a pedigree half a yard long, knocked down for two or three thousand guineas to some magnate of the turf, amidst the applause of the auction-yard.

'Elizabeth cannot fail to marry well, unless she behaves like an idiot, and throws herself away upon some pauper curate,' said Mrs. Chevenix: 'there is no position to which a girl with her advantages may not aspire—and I shall make it my business to give her plenty of opportunities—unless she is obstinately bent upon standing in her own light. This district-visiting business must be put a stop to immediately; it is nothing more than an excuse for flirting with that tall curate.'

Mrs. Chevenix was not slow to warn her brother, the Vicar, of this peril which menaced his handsomest daughter; but he, who was the easiest-tempered and least-designing of mankind, received her information with a provoking coolness.

'I really can't see how I could object to Lizzie's visiting the poor,' he said. 'It has always been a trouble to me that my daughters, with the exception of Gertrude, have done so little. If Forde has brought about a better state of things in this matter, as he has in a good deal besides, I don't see that I can complain of the improvement because it is his doing. And I don't think you need alarm yourself with regard to any danger of love-making or matrimony between those two. Forde has somewhat advanced notions, and doesn't approve of a priest marrying. He has almost said as much in the pulpit, and I think the Hawleigh girls have left off setting their caps at him.'

'Men are not always constant to their opinions,' said Mrs. Chevenix. 'I wouldn't give much for any declaration Mr. Forde may have made in the pulpit. It was very bad taste in him to advance any opinion of that kind, I think, when his vicar is a married man and the father of a family.'

'Forde belongs to the new school,' replied Mr. Luttrell, with his good-natured air. 'Perhaps he sometimes sails a trifle too near the wind in the matter of asceticism; but he's the best curate I ever had.'

'Why doesn't he go over to Rome, and have done

with it!' exclaimed aunt Chevenix angrily; 'I have no patience with such a wolf in sheep's clothing. And I have no patience with you, Wilmot, when I see your handsomest daughter throwing herself away before your eyes.'

'But I don't see anything of the kind, Maria,' said the Vicar, gently rolling his fingers round a cigar which he meant to smoke in the orchard so soon as he should escape from his tormentor. 'As to playing the spy upon my children—watching their flirtations with Jones, or speculating upon their penchant for Robinson, I think you ought to know by this time that I am the very last of men to do anything of that kind.'

'Which means in plain English that you are too selfish and too indifferent to trouble yourself about the fate of your daughters. You ought to have had sons, Wilmot; young scapegraces, who would have ruined you with university debts, or gone on the turf and dragged your name through the mire in that way.'

'I have not been blessed with sons,' murmured Mr. Luttrell in his laziest tone. 'If I had been favoured in that way, so soon as they arrived at an eligible age, I should have exported them. I should have obtained a government grant of land in Australia

or British Columbia, and planted them out. I consider emigration the natural channel for the disposal
of surplus sons.'

'You ought never to have married, Wilmot. You
ought to have been one of those dreadful abbots one
reads of, who had trout-streams running through
their kitchens, and devoted all the strength of their
minds to eating and drinking, and actually wallowed
in venison and larded capons.'

'Those ancient abbots had by no means a bad
time of it, my dear,' replied the Vicar, with supreme
good humour, 'and they had plenty of broken victuals
to feed their poor with, which I have not.'

'I want to know what you are going to do about
Elizabeth,' said Mrs. Chevenix, rapping the table
with her fan, and returning to the charge in a determined manner.

'What I am going to do about Elizabeth, my
love? Simply nothing. Would you have me lock
her up in the Norman tower, like a princess in a
fairy tale, so that she should not behold the face of
man till I chose to introduce her to a husband of my
own selection? All the legendary lore we possess
tends to show the futility of that sort of domestic
tyranny. I consider your apprehensions altogether
premature and groundless; but if it is Lizzie's

destiny to marry Malcolm Forde, I shall not interfere. He is a very good fellow, and he has some
private means, sufficient at any rate for the mainten-
ance of a wife: what more could I want?'

'And you would sacrifice such a girl as Elizabeth
to a Scotch curate,' said Mrs. Chevenix with the calm-
ness of despair. 'I always thought you were the
most short-sighted of mortals; but I did not believe
you capable of such egregious folly as this. That
girl might be a duchess.'

'Find me a duke, my dear Maria, and I will not
object to him for my son-in-law.'

Mrs. Chevenix sighed, and shook her head with a
despondent air; and Mr. Luttrell strolled out to the
orchard, leaving her to bewail his folly in confidential
converse with Diana, who in a manner represented
the worldly wisdom of the family.

'I wouldn't make such a fuss about Lizzie, if I
were you, auntie,' that young lady remarked somewhat coolly. 'I never knew a girl about whom her
people made too much fuss, setting her up as a
beauty, and so on, do anything wonderful in the way
of marriage.'

Like the eyes of the lynx, in his matchless
strength of vision, were the eyes of aunt Chevenix

for any sentimental converse between Elizabeth and Mr. Forde. It tortured her to know that they must needs have many opportunities of meeting outside the range of that keen vision—chance encounters in the cottages of the poor, or in the obscure lanes and alleys that fringed the chief street of Hawleigh. Vainly had she endeavoured to cajole her niece into the abandonment of those duties she had newly resumed. All her arguments, her flatteries, her ridicule, her little offerings of ribbons and laces and small trinketry, were wasted. After that visit of Malcolm Forde's the girl was constant to her work.

'It is such a happiness to feel that I can be of some use in the world, auntie,' she said, unconsciously repeating Mr. Forde's very words; 'and if you had seen how pleased all those poor souls were to see me amongst them again, you would hardly wonder at my liking the work.'

'A tribe of sycophants!' exclaimed Mrs. Chevenix contemptuously. 'I should like to know what value they'd attach to your visits, or how much civility they'd show you, if there were not tea and sugar, and coals and blankets in the background. And I should like to know how long you'd stick to your work if Mr. Forde had left Hawleigh?'

Elizabeth flamed crimson at this accusation, but

was not of a temper to be silenced by a hundred Chevenixes.

'Perhaps I might not like the work without his approval,' she said defiantly; 'but I hope I should go on with it all the same. I am not at all afraid to confess that his influence first set me thinking; that it was to please him I first tried to be good.'

'I am not an ultra-religious person, Elizabeth; but I should call that setting the creature above the Creator,' said Mrs. Chevenix severely. To which Lizzie muttered something that sounded like 'Bosh.'

'What else is there for me to do, I should like to know,' the girl demanded contemptuously, after an interval of silence, Mrs. Chevenix having retired within herself in a dignified sulkiness. 'Is there any amusement, or any excitement, or any distraction in our life in this place to hinder my devoting myself to these people?'

This speech was somewhat reassuring to Mrs. Chevenix: she inferred therefrom that if Elizabeth had had anything more agreeable to do, she would not have become a district-visitor.

'You have a fine voice, which you might cultivate to your future profit,' she said; 'a girl who sings really well is likely to make a great success in society.'

'I understand. One gets asked out to entertain

other people's friends; and one is not paid like a
professional singer. I like music well enough, aunt;
but you can't imagine I could spend half my existence
in shrieking solfeggi, even if papa would tolerate the
noise. I am sure, what with one and another of us,
the piano is jingling and clattering all day, as it is.
Papa and the servants must execrate the sound of it:
Blanche, with her *études de vélocité*, and Di with
her everlasting fugues and sonatas—it's something
abominable.'

'You might have a piano in your tower bedroom,
my dear. I wouldn't mind making you a present of
a cottage.'

'Thanks, auntie. Let it be a real cottage, then,
instead of a cottage piano—against I set up that love-
in-a-cottage you seem so much afraid of.'

'Upon my word, Elizabeth, I can never make
you out,' said Mrs. Chevenix plaintively. 'Sometimes I think you are a thoroughly sensible girl, and
at other times you really appear capable of any ab-
surdity.'

'Don't be frightened, auntie. It rather amuses
me to see your awe-stricken look when I say anything
peculiarly wild. But you need have no misgivings
about me. I am worldly-minded to the tips of my
nails, as the French say; and I am perfectly aware

that I am rather good-looking, and ought to make an advantageous marriage; only the eligible suitor is a long time appearing. Perhaps I shall meet him next spring in Eaton-place. As to Mr. Forde, he is quite out of the question. I know all about his past life, and know that he is a confirmed bachelor.'

'Your confirmed bachelors are a very dangerous race, Elizabeth,' said Mrs. Chevenix sententiously. 'They contrive to throw families off their guard by their false pretences, and generally end by marrying a beauty or an heiress. But I trust you have too much common sense to take up with a man who can barely afford to keep you.'

By such small doses of worldly-wise counsel did Mrs. Chevenix strive to fortify her niece against the peril of Malcolm Forde's influence. Her sharp eye had discovered something more than common kindliness in the Curate's bearing towards Elizabeth— something more than a mere spirit of contradiction in the girl's liking for him. But there was time enough yet, she told herself; and the tender sprout of passion might, by a little judicious management, be nipped in the bud. She would not even wait for the coming spring, she thought; but would carry off Elizabeth with her when she went back to town a little before Christmas. She had intended to spend that social season in a hospitable Wiltshire manor-house; but that visit might be deferred. Anything was better than to leave her niece exposed to the perilous influence of Malcolm Forde.

Again and again had she made a mental review of the tritons in the matrimonial market; or rather, of those special tritons who might be brought within the narrow waters of her own drawing-room, or could be encountered at will in that wider sea of society to which she had free ingress. There was Sir Rockingham Pendarvis, the rich Cornish baronet, whom it had been her privilege to meet at the dinner-parties of her own particular set, and who might be fairly counted upon for daily tea-drinking and occasional snug little dinners. There was Mr. Maltby, the great distiller, who had lately inherited a business popularly estimated at a hundred thousand a year. There was Mr. Miguel Zamires, the financier, with a lion's share in the public funds of various nations, aquiline-nosed and olive-skinned, speaking a peculiar Spanish-English with a somewhat guttural accent. These three were the mightier argosies that sailed upon society's smooth ocean; but there were numerous craft of smaller tonnage whereof Mrs. Chevenix kept a record, and any one of which would be a prize worth boarding.

Inscrutable are the decrees of the gods. While this diplomatic matron was weaving her web for the next London season—even planning her little dinners, reckoning the expenses of the campaign, resolving to do things with a somewhat lavish hand—Fate brought a nobler prize than any she had dared to dream of winning, and landed it, without effort of her own, at her feet.

CHAPTER VIII.

· He never saw, never before to-day,
What was able to take his breath away,
A face to lose youth for, to occupy age
With the dream of, meet death with—'

It was early in November, and Mrs. Chevenix had been at the Vicarage a month—a month of inexorable dulness, faintly relieved by a couple of provincial dinner-parties, at which the Hawleigh pastor assembled round his well-furnished board a choice selection of what were called the best people in the neighbourhood. But the best people seemed somewhat dismal company to Mrs. Chevenix, who cared for no society that lacked the real London flavour—the bouquet of Hyde-park and the Clubs. She was beginning to pine for the racier talk of her own peculiar set, for the small luxuries of her own establishment, when an event occurred which, in a moment, transformed Hawleigh, and rendered it just the most delightful spot upon this lower sphere.

She had gone to church with her nieces one Sun-

day morning in by no means a pleasant humour, cap-
tiously disposed rather, and inclined to hold forth
about their papa's peculiarities and their own shortcomings in a strain which Elizabeth openly resented,
and the other girls inwardly rebelled against.

'If I had been as cross as aunt Chevenix is this
morning in my nursery days, I should have been told
that I'd got up on the wrong side of my bed,' said
Blanche, walking with Diana in the rear of the matron.
'I suppose it wouldn't do for us mildly to suggest to
auntie that she must have got up on the wrong side
of her bed this morning.   It might seem out of
keeping.'

'I wonder you stop with us if our society is so
very unpleasant, aunt,' said Elizabeth boldly.

'You ungrateful girl! You ought to know that I
am staying in this relaxing climate, at the hazard of
my own health, simply in order to interpose my influence between you and destruction.'

Elizabeth greeted this reproach with a scornful
laugh, even at the gate of the churchyard.

'You foolish auntie! you surely don't suppose
that your presence here would prevent my doing anything I wished to do; that the mere dead-weight of
your worldly wisdom would quench the fire of my
impulses?' she said.

They were within the church-porch before aunt
Chevenix could reply. She sailed up the central aisle
with all her plain sails spread, and took the most
comfortable seat in the vicarage pew, without bestow-
ing so much as a glance upon the herd of nobodies
who worshipped their Creator in that remote temple,
and whose bonnets and choice of colours in general
she protested were barbarous enough to set her teeth
on edge.

She sat with half-closed eyelids and a languid air
during the earlier portion of the service, and kept her
seat throughout the reading of the Psalms; but in
the middle of the hymn that was sung before the
litany, Elizabeth was surprised by a complete change
in her aunt's manner. The cold blue eyes opened to
their widest extent, while their gaze grew fixed in an
eager stare. The carefully-finished eyebrows were
raised; the corners of the mouth, which feature had
previously been distinguished by a somewhat sour
expression, relaxed into a faint smile; the whole phy-
siognomy indicated at once pleasure and surprise.
The look was so marked that Elizabeth's eyes involuntarily followed the direction of her aunt's trans-
fixed gaze.

Her wondering glance that way did not show her
anything very strange—only old Lady Paulyn, a

somewhat faded dame, in a lavender satin bonnet, a
black velvet cloak, and rare old mechlin collar, all of
ancient fashion.   In precisely such garments could
Elizabeth remember Lady Paulyn from the days of
her childhood.   She lived in a huge and dismal architectural pile about seven miles from Hawleigh,
saw very little society, kept no state, and gave but
sparingly to the poor.   She had an only son, for
whom she was said to be hoarding her money, and
very large were the figures by which the gossips of
Hawleigh computed her hoards.

Of young Lord Paulyn (Viscount Paulyn in the
peerage of England, and Baron Ouchterlochy in Ire-
land), her only son, Hawleigh had of late years seen
so little that his face and figure were known to but
few among the denizens of that town.   But various
were the rumours of that young man's manners and
movements in the more brilliant scenes which he affected.   His tastes were of the turf, turfy; he was
said to have a tan gallop of his own at Newmarket,
and a stable in Yorkshire; and, while some authori-
ties declared that he was making ducks and drakes
of all the wealth of past generations of Paulyns—all
more or less distinguished by a miserly turn of mind,
and dating their nobility from the time of Charles
the Second, who, by way of recompense for divers

accommodations of a financial character, created one Jasper Paulyn, merchant and money-lender, Viscount Paulyn, of Ashcombe—other wiseacres affirmed that he had doubled his fortune by lucky transactions on the turf—betting against his own horses, and various strokes of genius of a like calibre.

On whichever side the truth may have lain, and whatever hazard there might be of future ruin, Lord Paulyn was, at this present date, accounted one of the richest bachelors in England. Mrs. Chevenix had met him on rare and happy occasions, to be remem· bered and boasted of long afterwards, and had gazed upon him with the eyes of worship. He had even been civil to her in his easy off-hand way, and had spoken of her to a common acquaintance as a 'decent old party;' 'held her head uncommon high, though, and looked as if she'd been driven with a bearing-rein.'

The Luttrells were on sufficiently friendly terms with the Viscount's mother, although the Viscount himself was a stranger to them. About twice a year Lady Paulyn called at the Vicarage, and about twice a year Mr. Luttrell and a brace of his daughters made a ceremonial visit to Ashcombe, the seat of the Paulyns. At school-treats and other charity festivals, on warm summer afternoons, the lavender satin bonnet would sometimes make its appearance, nodding to the commonalty with benignant condescension; while plethoric farmers of a radical turn opined that ' it 'ud be a deal better if the old gal 'ud put her name down for a fi'pun note a little oftener, instid o' waggling of her blessed old bonnet like a Chinee mandarin.'

Whatever five-pound notes Lady Paulyn did bestow upon the deserving or undeserving indigent were dealt out by the agency of Mr. Luttrell, or Mr. Chapman, the incumbent of an ancient little church in the ancient village of Ashcombe. No necessitous wanderers were allowed to prowl about the courtyards, or loiter at the backdoors of Ashcombe Manor. No dole of milk, or bread, or wine, or beer, or broken victuals, was ever dispensed in the Ashcombe kitchen. Lady Paulyn sold the produce of her dairy and poultry-yard, her garden stuffs and venison. Orchard-houses and vineries she had none, holding the cultivation of fruits under glass to be a new-fangled mode of wasting money, or she would assuredly have sold her grapes and pines and peaches. But she had acres of apple-orchard, whose produce she supplied to a cider manufacturer at Hawleigh, retaining only a certain number of bushels of the least saleable apples for the concoction of a peculiarly thin and acid liquor which she drank herself and gave to her servants and dependents.

'If it is good enough for me, my dear, it ought to be good enough for them,' she told her companion and poor relation, Miss Hilda Disney, when the voice of revolt was faintly heard from the servants' hall.

The lavender satin bonnet was not alone in the great square pew. Miss Disney was seated opposite her benefactress—a fair quiet-looking young woman, with long flaxen ringlets, and a curious stillness about her face and manner at all times; an air of supreme repose, which seemed to have grown up out of the solitude and silence of her joyless life until it had become an attribute of her own nature. She had refined and delicate features, a faultless complexion of the blended rose-and-lily order, large soft blue eyes, and lacked only life and expression to be almost beautiful. Wanting these, she was, in the words of Elizabeth Luttrell, a very pretty picture of a pink-and-white woman.

'There is not a factory girl in Hawleigh so much to be pitied as Miss Disney,' said Elizabeth, when she discovered this young lady's character and surroundings. 'How much better to be waxwork altogether than to be only half alive like that! But there is one advantage in having that kind of semi-sentient

nature. I don't believe Hilda Disney feels anything
—either the gloom of that dismal old house, or the
tyranny of that awful old woman. I don't suppose
she would mind very much if Lady Paulyn were to
stick pins in her, as the witches used to stick them
in *their* wax figures; or perhaps she might feel pins,
though she is impervious to nagging.'

To-day Elizabeth looked from the Viscountess to
Miss Disney, and wondered, with some touch of
feminine compassion, if she would ever have a new
bonnet, or go on wearing the same head-gear of
black lace and violets to her dying day. But there
was a third person in the Paulyn pew, and it was
upon the countenance of this last individual that the
distended eyeballs of Mrs. Chevenix gazed with that
gaze of wonderment and delight.

This third person was a stranger to the sight of
most people in Hawleigh. He was a man of about
six-and-twenty, broad shouldered and strongly built,
but not above the middle height, with a face that was
singularly handsome, after a purely animal type of
beauty — a low forehead; a short straight nose,
moulded rather than chiselled; full lips, shaded by
a thick brown moustache; a square jaw, a trifle too
heavy for the rest of the face; a powerful, column-
like throat, fully exposed by the low-cut collar, and

narrow strip of cravat; short-cut hair of reddish
brown; and large bright eyes of the same hue, a reddish hazel—eyes that had never been dimmed by
thought or study, but had something of the sailor's
hawk-like far-off vision. It was the face and figure
of a Greek athlete, the winner of the wild-olive crown,
in the days when strength was accounted beauty.

'Do you know who that is in the pew by the
altar?' whispered Mrs. Chevenix, under cover of the
tall green-baize-lined pew, when they knelt down for
the litany.

'Don't know, I'm sure,' replied Elizabeth indifferently; 'I suppose it's a stranger that they've put
into the Ashcombe pew.'

'That young man is Lord Paulyn, one of the
richest men in London,' said Mrs. Chevenix, in an
awe-stricken whisper.

'O,' said Elizabeth settling down to the responses,
and not peculiarly impressed by this announcement.

Sorely mechanical was Mrs. Chevenix's share in
the service after this discovery. Her lips murmured
the responses, with undeviating correctness. She
escaped every pitfall which our form of prayer offers
for the unwary, and came up to time at every point;
but her mind was busy with curious thoughts about
Lord Paulyn, and very little of the Vicar's good old

English sermon—a judicious solution of Tillotson, South, and Venn—found its way to her comprehension.

She contrived to steer her way down the aisle so as to emerge from the porch with her elbow against the elbow of Lord Paulyn, and then came radiant smiles of recognition, and intense astonishment at this unexpected meeting.

'There's nothing very remarkable in it,' said the Viscount, while the Luttrell girls were shaking hands with Lady Paulyn and Miss Disney; 'my mother lives down here, you know, and I generally come for a week or so in the huntin' season. Going to church is rather out of my line, I admit; but I sometimes do it here to gratify the mater. Any of your people live down here, Mrs. Chevenix?'

'Yes; I am staying with my brother, the Vicar.'

'Bless my soul! old Luttrell your brother, is he? I had no idea of that. Those girls belong to you, I suppose? rather nice girls—talking to my mother.'

'Those young ladies are my nieces.'

'Uncommonly handsome girl, that tall one. We're rather noted for that sort of thing in the west; pilchards, clotted cream, and fine women, are our staple. Pray introduce me to your nieces, Mrs. Chevenix. Do they hunt?'

Mrs. Chevenix shook her head despondently.

'Elizabeth has all the ambition for that kind of thing,' she said, 'but not the opportunity. My brother has four daughters, and the Church is not a Golconda.'

'That's a pity,' said the Viscount, staring at Elizabeth, who was talking to Miss Disney on the opposite side of the path, along which the congregation was slowly moving, with a good deal of nodding and becking and friendly salutation; 'that tall girl looks as if she'd be a straightish rider. I could give her a good mount, if her father would let her hunt.'

'That would be quite out of the question,' said Mrs. Chevenix; 'my brother has such strict notions;' a remark which might have sounded somewhat curious to the easy-going pastor himself; but Mrs. Chevenix had certain cards to play, and knew pretty well how to play them.

'Hump, I suppose so; a parson and all that kind of thing. Which is Elizabeth? The tall one?'

'Yes, Elizabeth is the tallest of the four.'

'She's an uncommonly handsome girl.'

'She is generally considered so.'

'Egad, so she ought to be. There wasn't a girl to compare with her in this year's betting. Introduce me, please, Mrs. Chevenix.'

The matron hesitated, as if this demand were hardly agreeable to her. ' I think the introduction would come better from Lady Paulyn,' she said, ' as my nieces appear to be on friendly terms with her.'

' O, very well; my mother can present me—it comes to the same thing. Don't you know her?'

Mrs. Chevenix shook her head with a gentle melancholy.

' My nieces have not taken the trouble to make us acquainted,' she said; ' I was not even aware that Lady Paulyn had a seat in this part of the country.'

She might have added, that she was not even aware of Lady Paulyn's existence until this morning. She had supposed the Viscount to be in the independent position of an orphan.

' O, yes, we've a place down here, and a precious ugly one, but my mother likes it; doesn't cost much to keep up, though it's big enough for a barrack. I say, mother,' crossing the pathway, which was now nearly clear, ' this is Mrs. Chevenix, Mr. Luttrell's sister, who is dying to know you.'

Mrs. Chevenix made a sweeping curtsey, as if she had some idea of subsiding into unknown depths below the timeworn tombstones that paved the pathway. The lavender bonnet gave a little friendly nod, and the Viscountess extended a paw in a crumpled black kid glove.

'And now, mother, you may present me to these young ladies,' said the Viscount.

The presentation was made, but hardly with that air of cordiality which it was Lady Paulyn's habit to employ as a set-off against the closeness of her financial operations and the inhospitality of her gaunt old mansion. Mrs. Chevenix detected a lurking reluctance in the dowager's manner of making her son known to the Luttrell girls.

The Vicar came out of the porch while this ceremony was being performed, with Malcolm Forde by his side. There were more greetings, and Elizabeth had time to shake hands with her father's curate, although Lord Paulyn was in the very utterance of some peculiarly original remark about the general dulness of Hawleigh. Mr. Forde had been very kind to her since her return to the path he had chalked out for her—deferential even in his manner, as if she had become at once the object of his gratitude and respect. But he had no opportunity of saying much to Elizabeth just now, though she had turned at once to greet him, and had forgotten to respond to Lord Paulyn's remark about Hawleigh; for Gertrude

plunged immediately into the usual parish talk, and
held forth upon the blessed fruits of her late labours
as manifest in the appearance of a certain Job Smi-
thers in the free seats: 'A man who was almost an
infidel, dear Mr. Forde, and used to take his children's Sunday-frocks to the pawnbroker's every Thursday or Friday, in order to obtain drink. But I
am thankful to say I persuaded him to take the
pledge, and I cherish hopes of his complete reforma-
tion.'

'Rather given to pledges, that fellow, I should
think, Miss Luttrell,' said the Viscount, in an ir-
reverent spirit. 'I can't conceive why young ladies in
the country plague themselves with useless attempts
at reforming such fellows. I don't believe there's a
ha'porth of good done by it. You may keep a man
sober for a week, but he'll break out and drink double as much for the next fortnight. You might as
well try to stop a man from having scarlet-fever when
the poison's in his blood. I had a trainer, now, in
the north, as clever a fellow as ever breathed. I
think if you'd given him a clothes-horse to train,
he'd have made it win a cup before he'd done with it.
But there was no keeping him away from the bottle.
I tried everything; talked to him like a father, supplied him with château Lafitte, to try and get him

off brandy; but it was no use, and the stupid beggar had one attack of D. T. after another, till he went off his head altogether, and had to be locked up.'

This improving anecdote Lord Paulyn apparently related for the edification of Elizabeth; since, although he began by addressing Gertrude, it was on the younger sister his gaze was fixed, as he dwelt plaintively on the hapless doom of his trainer.

'Won't you come to the Vicarage for luncheon, Lady Paulyn?' asked Mr. Luttrell, who had the old-fashioned eager country-squireish hospitality, and who saw that the Viscount hardly seemed inclined to move from his stand upon a crumbling old tombstone which recorded the decease of 'Josiah Judd of this parish; also of Amelia Judd, wife of the above; and of Hannah, infant daughter of the above,' and so on, through a perplexing string of departed Judds, all of this parish; a fact dwelt upon with as much insistence as if to be 'of this parish' were an earthly distinction that ought to prove a passport to eternal felicity.

'You're very kind,' said the dowager graciously, 'and your luncheons are always excellent; but I shouldn't like to have the horses out so late on a Sunday, and Parker, my coachman, is a Primitive Methodist, and makes a great point of attending his own chapel once every Sunday. I like to defer to my servants' prejudices in these small matters.'

'O Lady Paulyn, I hope you don't call salvation a small matter!' ejaculated Gertrude, who would have lectured an archbishop.

'Hang Parker's prejudices!' cried Lord Paulyn; 'and as to those two old screws of yours in the chariot, I don't believe anything could hurt them. They ought to have been sent to a knacker's yard five years ago. I always call that wall-eyed gray the Ancient Mariner. He holds me with his glassy eye. We'll come to the Vicarage, by all means, Mr. Luttrell.'

The dowager gave way at once. She was much too wise to make any attempt at dragooning this only son, for whose enrichment she had pinched and scraped and hoarded until pinching and scraping and hoarding had become the habit of her mind. Too well did she know that Reginald Paulyn was a young man who would go his own way; that her small economies, her domestic cheese-paring, and flint-skinning were as so many drops of water as compared with the vast ocean of his expenditure. Yet she went on economising with ineffable patience, and thought no day ill-spent in which she had saved a shilling between sunrise and sunset.

They all moved away in the direction of the Vicarage, which, unlike the usual run of vicarages, was somewhat remote from the church.

There was a walk of about a quarter of a mile between St. Clement's, which stood just within the West Bar, a gray old archway at the end of the highstreet, and the abode of the Luttrells. The Vicar offered his arm to the dowager.

'You'll come with us, of course, Forde,' he said, in his friendly way, looking round at his curate, and the curate did not refuse that offer of hospitality.

Sunday luncheon at Hawleigh Vicarage was a famous institution. Mr. Luttrell, as a rule, abjured that mid-day meal, pronouncing it, in the words of some famous epicure, 'an insult to a man's breakfast, and an injury to his dinner.' But on Sunday the pastor sacrificed himself to the convenience of his household, and went without his seven-o'clock dinner, in order that his cook might exhibit her best bonnet in the afternoon and evening at his two churches. There was no roasting or boiling in the vicarage kitchen on that holy day, only a gentle simmering of curries and fricassees, prepared overnight; nor was there any regular dinner, but by way of substitute therefor, a high tea at eight o'clock, a pleasant easy-

going banquet, which had been much affected by
former curates.   But woe be to the household if the
two-o'clock luncheon were not a select and savoury
repast! and Miss Luttrell and the cook held solemn
consultation every Saturday morning in order to
secure this result.

So the Vicar enjoyed himself every Sunday with
his friends round him, and bemoaned himself every
Monday on the subject of that untimely meal, declar-
ing that he had thrown his whole internal machinery
out of gear for the accommodation of his servants.

To-day the luncheon seemed a peculiar success.
Lady Paulyn, who was somewhat a stranger to the
good things of this life, did ample justice to the
viands, devoured curried chicken with the gusto of an
Anglo-Indian, called the parlour-maid back to her
for a second supply of oyster vol-au-vent, and wound-
up with cold sirloin and winter salad, in a manner
that was eminently suggestive of indigestion.   Lord
Paulyn had the modern appetite, which is of the
weakest, trifled with a morsel of curry, drank a good
deal of seltzer-and-brandy, and enjoyed himself amaz-
ingly after his manner, entertaining Elizabeth, by
whose side he had contrived to be seated, with the
history of his Yorkshire stable, and confiding to her
his lofty hopes for the coming year.

She was not particularly interested in this agreeable discourse; but she could see, just as plainly as Mrs. Chevenix saw, that the Viscount was impressed by her beauty, and it was not un-pleasant to her to have made such an impression upon that patrician mind, even if it were merely the affair of an hour. Nor was she unconscious of a certain steady watchfulness in the dark deep-set eyes of Malcolm Forde, who sat opposite to her, and was singularly inattentive to the remarks of his next neighbour, Gertrude.

'I don't suppose his perfect woman ever had the opportunity of flirting with a viscount,' thought Elizabeth, 'or that she would have done such a thing if she had. I like to horrify him with an occasional glimpse of these depths of iniquity to which *I* can descend. If he cared for me a little, now, and there were any chance of making him jealous, the pleasure would be ever so much keener; but that is out of the question.'

So the reformed Elizabeth, the Christian pastor's daughter, who visited the poor, and comforted the af-flicted, and supported the heads of sick children on her bosom, and read the gospel to the ignorant, and did in some vague undeterminate manner struggle towards the higher, purer life, vanished altogether,

giving place to a young person who improved her
opportunity with the Viscount as dextrously as if
she had been bred up at the knees of aunt Chevenix, and had never known any loftier philosophy
than that which dropped from those worldly lips.
Malcolm Forde looked on, and shuddered. 'And for
such a woman I had almost been false to the memory
of Alice Fraser!'

It must not be supposed that Elizabeth's iniquity
was of an outrageous nature. She was only listening
with an air of profound interest to Lord Paulyn's
stable-talk, even trying to comprehend the glory of
possessing a horse entered for next year's Derby,
about which fifteen to two had been freely taken at
Manchester during the autumn, and who was likely
to advance in the betting after Christmas. She was
only smiling radiantly upon a young man she had
never seen until that morning—only receiving the
homage of admiring eyes with a gracious air of
unconsciousness; like some splendid flower which
does not shrink or droop under the full blaze of a
meridian sun, but rather basks and brightens beneath the glory of the sun-god.

But to the eyes of the man who watched her with
an interest he would have hardly cared to confess to
himself, this conduct seemed very black indeed.

He groaned inwardly over the defection of this fair young soul, which not a little while ago he had deemed regenerate.

'She is not worth the anxiety I feel about her,' he said to himself: 'Gertrude is a hundred times her superior, really earnest, really good, not a creature of whim and impulse, drifted about by every wind that blows. And yet I cannot feel the same interest in her.'

And then he began to wonder if there were indeed something inherently interesting in sin, and if the repentant sinner must needs always have the advantage of the just person. It seemed almost a hard saying to him, that touching sentence of the gospel of hope, which reserves its highest promises for the wilful, passionate soul that has chosen its own road in life and has only been brought home broken, and soiled, and tarnished at the last.

Gertrude was virtuous, but not interesting. Vainly did Malcolm Forde endeavour to apply his ear to her discourse. His attention was distracted, in spite of himself, by that animated talk upon the other side of the wide oval table ; his eyes wandered now to the handsome, sensual face of the Viscount, now to Elizabeth's lively countenance, which expressed no weariness of that miserable horsey talk. Nor was

Mr. Forde the only person present who took note of that animated conversation.

From her place at the farther end of the table, Miss Disney's calm blue eyes wandered ever and anon towards her kinsman and Elizabeth, hardly with any show of interest or concern, but with a coldly curious air, as if she wondered at Lord Paulyn's vivacity, as an unwonted exhibition on his part. She was very quiet, spoke little, and only replied in the briefest sentences to any remark made by Mr. Luttrell, next to whom she was seated. She ate hardly anything, rarely smiled, and appeared to take very little more interest in the life about and around her than if she had been, indeed, a waxen image, impervious to pain or pleasure.

Luncheon came to an end at last, after being drawn out to a point that seemed intolerable to the Curate; · St. Mary's bells sounded in the distance, from the eastern end of the large straggling town. There was only a short afternoon service; the litany and a catechising of the children, which Mr. Luttrell himself rarely attended, deeming that perambulatory examination of small scholars, the hearing of collect, epistle, and gospel, stumbled through with more or less blundering by monotonous treble voices, a task peculiarly adapted to the curate mind. So, as soon as grace had been said, Mr. Forde rose quietly, shook hands with Gertrude, and slipped away, not unseen by Elizabeth. 'There's a good deal of that fellow for a curate,' said Lord Paulyn, casting a lazy glance at the retreating figure; 'he ought to have been a life-guardsman.'

'Mr. Forde has been in the army,' Elizabeth answered coldly.

'I thought as much, and in a cavalry regiment, of course. He has the "long sword, saddle, bridle" walk. What made him take to the Church? The army's bad enough—stiff examinations, bad pay, hard work; but it must be better than the Church. What made him change his profession?'

'Mr. Forde has not taken the trouble to acquaint the world with his motives,' said Elizabeth with increasing coldness.

Lord Paulyn looked at her curiously. She seemed somewhat sensitive upon the subject of this tall curate. Was there anything between them, he wondered; a flirtation, an engagement even perhaps. He had caught the Curate's glance wandering her way several times during the banquet.

'Egad, the fellow has good taste,' thought Lord Paulyn. 'She's the prettiest woman I ever saw, bar none, and is no end too good for a snuffling parson.

I'll make that old Chevenix tell me all about it presently.'

'That old Chevenix' had been trying to make her way with the dowager during the lengthy meal, entertaining her with little scraps of town-talk and small lady-like scandal; not virulent vulgar slander, but good-natured genial kind of gossip, touching lightly upon the failings and errors of one's acquaintance, deploring their little infirmities and mistaken courses with a friendly compassionate spirit, essentially Christian. But she was mortified to discover that her small efforts to amuse were futile. The dowager would not acknowledge acquaintance with one of the people Mrs. Chevenix talked about, or the faintest interest in those public characters, the shining lights of the great world, about whose private life every well-regulated British mind is supposed to be curious.

'I don't know her,' said this impracticable old woman; 'I never met him; I'm not acquainted with 'em;' until the soul of the Chevenix sank within her, for she was ardently desirous of establishing friendly relations with this perverse dowager.

'I'm a Devonshire woman, and I only know Devonshire people,' said the dowager, ruthlessly cutting short one of the choicest stories that had been current in the last London season.

'Then you must know the Trepethericks!' exclaimed Mrs. Chevenix, in her gushing way; 'dear Lady Trepetherick is a sweet woman, and one of my best friends; and Sir Charles, what a thorough independent-minded Englishman!'

'I never heard of 'em,' replied the dowager bluntly; and Mrs. Chevenix was hardly sorry when the conclusion of the meal brought her hopeless endeavours to a close.

'I can't keep those horses waiting any longer,' said this ungrateful old woman, as she rose from the table, after having eaten to repletion. 'Will you tell them to bring my carriage directly, Reginald?'

'Nonsense, mother; the horses are in the stable, and much better off than they'd be at Ashcombe, I daresay,' answered the Viscount: 'I'm not coming home for an hour. Miss Luttrell is going to show me the garden, and an ancient turret that was part of Hawleigh Castle.'

'Miss Luttrell is at the other end of the room,' said the dowager grimly, perceiving that her son's gaze was rooted to Elizabeth.

'Miss Elizabeth Luttrell, then,' said that young man; 'you'll show me the garden, won't you?'

'There's not much worth your looking at,' answered Elizabeth carelessly.

'O, yes, there is: a man would travel a long way
to see as much,' cried the Viscount significantly; and
then thinking that his admiration had been somewhat too direct, he went on—'a mediæval tower, you
know, and all that kind of thing. But you needn't
wait for me, mother, if you're really anxious to get
home. I'll find my way back to Ashcombe somehow.'

'What, walk seven miles between this and dinner-
time!' exclaimed the dowager.

'There are circumstances under which a man
might do as much,' answered the Viscount; 'and the
Ashcombe dinners are not banquets which I hold in
extreme reverence.'

Lady Paulyn sighed despondently. It was a hard
thing to have toiled for such an ingrate.

'I'll wait for you, Reginald,' she said with a re-
signed air. 'Parker must lose his afternoon service
for once in a way. I daresay he'll give me warning
to-morrow morning.'

So Lord Paulyn went into the garden with Elizabeth, longing sorely for the solacement of a cigar,
even in that agreeable society. He made the circuit
of grounds in which there was very little to see in the
month of November; went into the orchard, which he
pronounced 'rather a jolly little place,' and contem-

plated the landscape to be seen therefrom; examined the moss-grown tower which flanked the low white house, and uttered divers critical remarks which did not show him to be a profound student of archæology.

'Nice old place for a smoking crib,' he said: 'what do you use it for? lumber-room, or coal or wine cellar—eh?'

'My sister Blanche and I sleep in it,' replied Elizabeth, laughing: 'I wouldn't change my tower-room for any other in the house.'

'Ah, but you'll change it, you know, one of these days when you have a house of your own; and such a girl as you must look forward to something better than this old Vicarage.'

'I am quite satisfied with surroundings that are good enough for the rest of my family,' said Elizabeth with her proudest air; 'and I have never looked forward to anything of the kind.'

'O, but, come now, really, you know,' remonstrated the Viscount, 'a girl like you can't mean to be buried alive for ever. You ought to see the world —Ascot, you know, and Goodwood, and the Oxford and Cambridge boat-race, and the pigeon-shooting at Hurlingham. You can't intend to mope in this dreary old place all your life. I don't mean to say anything against your father's house, and I'm sure he gave us an uncommonly good luncheon; but this kind of life is not up to *your* mark, you know.'

Here was a second counsellor suggesting that the life Elizabeth Luttrell lived was not good enough for her, urging upon her the duty of rising above her surroundings; but in a somewhat different spirit from that other adviser, whom she had of late pretended to obey. And this foolish impressionable soul was but too ready to follow the new guide, too ready to admit that it was a hard thing to be fettered to the narrow life of a country parsonage, to be cut off for ever from that brighter world of Ascot and Goodwood. It was not that she considered the Viscount at all a superior person. She was quite able to perceive that this heir of all the ages and all the Paulyns was made of very vulgar clay; but she knew that he was a power in that unknown world whose pleasures she had sometimes longed for with an intense longing, and it was not unpleasant to hear from so great an authority that she was worthy to shine there.

She was not alone with the Viscount in the garden even for half an hour. The proprieties must be observed in Devonshire as well as in Belgravia. Mrs. Chevenix was taking a constitutional with Diana close at hand, while Elizabeth and the lordling were strolling along the garden walks, and making the circuit of the orchard. The dowager had also hobbled out by this time, with Mr. Luttrell in attendance upon her, not too well pleased at being cut off from the sweets of his afternoon nap.

'I might as well be catechising the children as doing this,' he thought dolefully. But there is an end of all social self-sacrifice, and the lumbering old yellow chariot came grinding over the carriage drive at last, whereupon Lady Paulyn declared that she *must* go.

'I am sure we have had a vastly agreeable visit,' she said, wagging her ancient head graciously, and softening at her departure with a grateful recollection of that toothsome vol-au-vent; 'you must all come and dine with me one of these days.' This was a vague kind of invitation, which the Luttrells had heard before; a shadowy coin, wherewith the dowager paid off small obligations.

'Yes, mother,' cried Lord Paulyn eagerly; 'you'd better ask Mr. Luttrell and the young ladies, and —er—Mrs. Chevenix to dine with you some day next week, while I'm at Ashcombe, you know. It's deuced dull there unless we're lucky enough to get nice people. What day will suit you, eh, Mr. Luttrell?'

'Hilda shall write Miss Luttrell a little note,' said

the dowager graciously; 'Hilda writes all my little notes.'

'Notes be hanged!' exclaimed Lord Paulyn; 'why not settle it now? You are not going to give a party, you know; you never do. Come, Luttrell, name your day for bringing over the young ladies. There'll be nobody to meet you, unless it's Chapman, the Ashcombe parson, a very good fellow, and an uncommonly straight rider. Will Thursday suit you? that's an off-day with me. You might come over to luncheon, and do the family pictures, if you care about that dingy school of art;—couldn't you?' this to Elizabeth.

'The Miss Luttrells have seen our picture-gallery, Reginald,' said the dowager.

'Well, never mind, they can see it again. I know those old portraits—a collection of ancient mugs—are not much worth looking at; but in the country, you know, one must do something; it's a good way of getting through a winter's afternoon. And I can teach you bézique, if you don't know it'—this to the damsels generally, but with a special glance at Elizabeth. 'We'll say Thursday then, at two o'clock; and mind, we shall expect you all, sha'n't we, mother?'

He hoisted her into the chariot before she could

gainsay him, and in a manner extinguished her and
any objection she might have been disposed to
offer.

'What a charming young man!' exclaimed Mrs.
Chevenix, as the chariot rumbled away, after very
cordial adieux from the Viscount, and a somewhat
cold leave-taking from Hilda Disney. 'So frank, so
easy, so unassuming, so utterly unconscious of his
position; one would never discover from his manner
that he was one of the richest noblemen in England,
and that the Paulyns are as old a family as the
Percys.'

'I don't see any special merit in that,' said Mr.
Luttrell, laughing; 'a man can hardly go about the
world labelled with the amount of his income, or wear
his genealogical tree embroidered upon the back of
his coat. And you're mistaken when you call the
Paulyns a good old family. They were in trade as
late as the reign of Charles the Second, and owe their
title to the king's necessities. The young fellow is
well enough, however, and seems good-natured and
friendly; but I cannot say that the manners of the
present day impress me by their elegance or their
polish, if I am to take Lord Paulyn as a fair sample
of your modern fine gentleman.'

'The fine gentleman is as extinct as the megatherium, **Wilmot; he went out** with high collars and black-satin stocks.   The qualities we appreciate nowadays are ease and savoir-faire.   If poor George the Fourth could **come to** life again, with his grand manner, what an absurd creature we **should** all think the first gentleman of Europe!'

'I am sorry for our modern taste, then, my dear,' answered the Vicar; 'but as Lord Paulyn seems inclined to be civil, I suppose we must make the best of him.   I wish he'd spend more of his time down here, and keep up the old house as it ought to be kept, for the good of the neighbourhood.'

'O you blind old mole!' thought Mrs. Chevenix, as Mr. Luttrell retired to his den; a little bit of a room at the end of the house, with a latticed window looking down upon the sloping orchard; a window that faced the western sun, and warmed the room pleasantly upon a winter afternoon.   There was a tiny fireplace in a corner; a capacious arm-chair; a writing-table, at which the **Vicar** hammered out his weekly sermon when he treated his congregation to a new one; a battered old bookcase, containing a few books of reference, and Mr. Luttrell's college classics, with the cribs that had assisted him therewith. Here he was wont to slumber peacefully on a Sabbath afternoon until Blanche brought him a **cup of strong** tea, and told him it was time to think about evening service.

Mrs. Chevenix ensconced herself in her favourite chair by the drawing-room fire, with a banner-screen carefully adjusted for the protection of her complexion, and sat for a long time slowly fanning herself, and meditating on the events of the day. That Lord Paulyn was impressed by her niece's beauty—in modern phraseology, hard hit—the astute widow had no doubt; but on the other hand he might be a young man who was in the habit of being hard hit by every pretty girl he met, and the impression might result in nothing. Yet that invitation to Ashcombe, about which he had shown such eagerness, indicated something serious. It might be a question of time, perhaps. If the young man stayed long enough in the neighbourhood, there was no saying what brilliant result might come of the admiration which he had exhibited to-day with such a delightful candour.

'How very odd that you should never have seen Lord Paulyn before, Blanche!' said Mrs. Chevenix to her youngest niece, who was sitting on the hearthrug making believe to read a volume of Sunday literature.

'It's not particularly odd, auntie, for he very

seldom comes here; and when he does come—about once in two years perhaps—it's only for the hunting. I never saw him in church before to-day, that I can remember.'

'But it is still more strange that I should never have heard you speak of his mother.'

'O, she's a stingy old thing, and we don't any of us care for her. We only see her about twice a year, and there's no reason we should talk about her. She's a most uninteresting old party.'

'My dearest Blanche, ease of manner is one thing, and vulgarity is another; I wish you would bear in mind that distinction. Party, except in its legal or collective sense, is a word I abhor; and a girl of your age would do well to adopt a more respectful tone in speaking of your superiors in the social scale.'

'I really can't be respectful about old Lady Paulyn, aunt. We had a housemaid from Ashcombe; and, O, the stories she told me about that dreadful house! They'd make your hair stand on end. I wonder what they'll give us for dinner next Thursday. Barleybroth perhaps, and boiled leg of mutton.'

'Blanche, I beg that you will desist from such flippant chatter. Lady Paulyn may be eccentric, but she is a lady whose notice it is an honour to receive.

Do you know how long Lord Paulyn usually stays at Ashcombe?'

'He doesn't usually stay there, aunt. He has been there once in two years, as far as I know; and has stayed for a fortnight or three weeks. I've heard people say that he cares for nothing but horses, and that he spends his life in going from one race-meeting to another.'

'A thorough Englishman's taste,' said Mrs. Chevenix approvingly. If she had been told that he was an amateur housebreaker, or had a passion for garrotting, she would have hardly blamed his weakness. 'But I have no doubt he will give up that sort of thing when he marries.'

CHAPTER IX.

' The burden of sweet speeches. Nay, kneel down,
　　Cover thy head, and weep; for verily
These market-men that buy thy white and brown
　　In the last days shall take no thought for thee.
In the last days like earth thy face shall be,
　　Yea, like sea-marsh made thick with brine and mire,
Sad with sick leavings of the sterile sea.
　　This is the end of every man's desire.'

THE Vicar had fully expected to receive one of Miss
Disney's little notes postponing the dinner at Ashcombe, so foreign was it to the manners and customs
of the dowager to extend so much hospitality to her
neighbours; but instead of the little note of post-
ponement there came a little note ' to remind ;' and,
as Mr. Luttrell observed, with an air of resignation,
there was nothing for it but to go.

Then came a grand consultation as to who should
go. It was not to be supposed that Mr. Luttrell
could enter society, even in the most friendly way,
with five women in his wake. Gertrude at once

announced her indifference to the entertainment. It was Thursday, and on that night there was an extra service and a sermon at St. Clement's. She would not lose Mr. Forde's sermon for the world.

'And I should think *you* would hardly miss that, Lizzie,' she said, 'since you have become so stanch a Forde-ite.'

But on this Mrs. Chevenix protested vehemently that Elizabeth must go to Ashcombe. She had been especially mentioned by the Viscount. He was to teach her bézique.

'I know all about bézique already, and I hate it,' Elizabeth answered coolly; 'but I should like to see a dinner at Ashcombe. I want to see whether it will be all make-believe, like the Barmecide's feast, or whether there will really be some kind of food upon the table. My impression is, that the dinner will consist of a leg of mutton and an epergne.'

It was decided therefore, after a little skirmishing between the sisters, that Elizabeth and Diana should accompany Mr. Luttrell and Mrs. Chevenix to Ashcombe, and that Gertrude and Blanche should stay at home. The vicarage wagonette, which had a movable cover that transformed it into a species of genteel baker's cart, would hold four very comfortably. The Vicar could afford to absent himself for once in a way from the Thursday-evening service, which was an innovation of Mr. Forde's.

The appointed day was not altogether unpropitious, but was hardly inviting : a dull dry winter day, with a gray sunless sky and a north-east wind, which whistled shrilly among the leafless elms and beeches of the wide avenue in Ashcombe Park as the vicarage wagonette drove up to the house.

Ashcombe Park was a great tract of low-lying land, stretched at the feet of a rugged hill that rose abruptly from the very edge of the wide lawn on one side of the house, and overshadowed it with its gaunt outline like a couchant giant. The mansion itself was a triumph of that school of architecture in which the research of ugliness seems to have been the directing principle of the designer's mind. It was a huge red-and-yellow brick edifice of the Vanbrugh school, with a ponderous centre and more ponderous wings ; long ranges of narrow windows unrelieved by a single ornament ; broad flights of shallow stone steps on each side of the tall central door ; a garden-door at the end of each wing ; an inner quadrangle, embellished with a hideous equestrian statue of some distinguished Paulyn who had perished at Malplaquet : a house which, in better occupation and with lighter surroundings, might not have been without a certain old-fashioned dignity and charm of its own peculiar order, but which in the possession of Lady Paulyn wore an aspect of depressing gloom.

There were some darksome specimens of the conifer tribe in huge square wooden tubs upon the broad gravelled walk before the principal front; but there was no pretence of a flower-garden on any side of the mansion. Lady Paulyn abjured floriculture as a foolish waste of money. The geometrical flower-beds in the Dutch garden, that had once adorned the south wing, had been replaced by a flat expanse of turf, on which her ladyship's sheep ranged at their pleasure; the wide lawn before the grand saloon—a panelled chamber of fifty feet long, with musical instruments and emblems painted in medallions on the panels—was also a pasture for those useful animals, which sometimes gazed through the narrow panes of windows, with calm wondering eyes, while Lady Paulyn and Hilda sat at work within.

Lord Paulyn was pacing the walk by the conifers as the wagonette drove up, and flew to assist the vicarage man-of-all-work in his attendance upon the ladies.

'I'm so glad you've all come,' he exclaimed, as he handed out Elizabeth, apparently unconscious of the absence of her two sisters. 'Very good of your

father to bring you to such a dismal hole. I sometimes wonder my mother and Hilda don't go to sleep
for a hundred years like the girl in the fairy tale,
from sheer inability to get rid of their time in any
other way. But they sit and stitch, stitch, stitch,
like a new version of the Song of the Shirt, and write
letters to distant friends, the Lord knows what about.
Here, Treby, take care of the ladies' wraps, will you,'
he said to a feeble old man in a threadbare suit of
black, who was my lady's butler and house-steward,
and was popularly supposed to clean the knives and
fill the coal-scuttles in a cavernous range of cellars
with which the mansion was undermined.

The Viscount led the way to the drawing-room,
or saloon—that spacious apartment with the flesh-
coloured panelling which had been originally designed
for a music-room. It was a stately chamber, with six
long windows, and two fireplaces with high narrow
mantelpieces, upon each of which appeared a scanty
row of tiny Nankin tea-cups. Scantiness was indeed
the distinguishing feature of the Ashcombe furniture
from garret to cellar, but was perhaps more strikingly
obvious in this spacious apartment than in any other
room in the house. A faded and much-worn Turkey
carpet covered the centre of the floor—a mere island
in an ocean of bees-waxed oak; a few spindle-legged

chairs and tables were dotted about here and there; two hard-seated couches of the classic mould—their frames rosewood inlaid with brass, their cushions covered with a striped satin damask, somewhat frayed at the edges, and exhibiting traces of careful repair—stood at a respectful distance from each fireplace; and one easy-chair, of a more modern manufacture, but by no means a choice or costly specimen of the upholsterer's art, was drawn close up to the one hearth upon which there burned a somewhat meagre pile of small wood, the very waste and refuse of the timber-yard. Lady Paulyn was seated in this chair, with a little three-cornered shawl of her own knitting drawn tightly round her skinny shoulders, as if she would thereby have eked out the sparing supply of fuel. Miss Disney sat at one of the little tables remote from the fire, copying a column of figures into an account-book. Both ladies rose to receive their guests, but not with a rapturous greeting.

'It's very good of you to come all this way to see a quiet old woman like me,' said the dowager, as if she had hardly expected them, in spite of Hilda's note 'to remind.'

'Why the deuce don't you have a fire in both fireplaces in such weather as this, mother?' the Viscount demanded, shivering, as he placed himself on the centre of the hearthrug, and thus obscured the only fire there was.

'I never have had two fires in this room, Reginald, and I never will have two fires,' replied the dowager resolutely. 'When I can't sit here with one fire, I shall leave off sitting here altogether. I don't hold with your modern luxurious habits.'

'But it must have been an ancient habit to warm this room a little better than you do, or it would hardly have been built with two fireplaces,' said Lord Paulyn.

'That, I imagine, was rather a question of architectural uniformity,' replied the dowager.

'There's the luncheon-gong,' said her son. 'Perhaps we shall find it a little warmer in the dining-room.'

There was a good deal of ceremony at Ashcombe, considering the scantiness of the household; and Lady Paulyn took no refreshment that was not heralded by beat of gong. Her little bit of roast mutton, or her fried sole and skinny chicken, cost no more on account of that majestic prelude, and it kept up the right tone, as my lady sometimes observed to Hilda. The luncheon to-day, though quite a festive banquet in comparison with the silver biscuit-barrel and mouldering Stilton cheese which formed the staple of the daily meal, was not too bountiful a repast. There was a gaunt piece of ribs of beef, bony and angular, as of an ox that had known hard times, at one end of the long table; a melancholy-looking roast fowl, with huge and scaly legs, whose advanced age ought to have held him sacred from the assassin, and who seemed to feel his isolated position on a very large dish, with a distant border of sliced tongue, lemon, and parsley. There were two dishes of potatoes, fried and boiled; there was a little glass dish of marmalade, that was made quite a feature of on one side of the board; and a similar dish containing six anchovies reposing in a grove of parsley, which enlivened the other side. There was an artistic preparation of beetroot and endive on a centre dish, and two ponderous diamond-cut celery glasses scantily supplied with celery; these, with a pickle-stand or two, and a good deal of splendour in the way of cruets, gave the table an air of being quite liberally furnished.

The meal was tolerably cheerful despite a certain toughness and wooden flavour in the viands. Mr. Luttrell pleaded his sworn enmity to luncheons as an excuse for not eating anything; and conversed agreeably with the dowager, who had brightened a little by this time, and seemed determined to make

the best of things. Lord Paulyn sat between Mrs.
Chevenix and Elizabeth, and had a good deal to say
for himself in one way or another. He was enchanted
to hear that Elizabeth was to have a season in town
next year.

‘You must come to me for the Oxford and Cambridge, mind, Mrs. Chevenix,’ he said. ‘I always
charter a crib—I beg your pardon—take a house on
the river for that event. I thought Miss Elizabeth
would never consent to be buried alive down here all
her days. She isn’t like my mother and Hilda. It
suits them very well. There’s something of the fossil
in their composition, and a century or so more or
less in a pit doesn’t make any difference to them.
I’m so glad I shall see you in town next year.’

This to Elizabeth, and with an extreme hearti-
ness. He could hardly behave like this to every
pretty girl he met, Mrs. Chevenix thought; it must
mean something serious; and in the dim future she
beheld herself allied to the peerage, through her niece,
Lady Paulyn.

The Viscount seemed very glad when luncheon
was over, and he could carry off the two young ladies
to see the family portraits.

‘ You won’t care much about that kind of thing, I
daresay,’ he said to Mrs. Chevenix, not caring to be

troubled with that matron's society; 'you'd rather stop and talk to my mother.'

'There is nothing would give me more pleasure than a chat with dear Lady Paulyn,' simpered aunt Chevenix, inwardly shuddering as she remembered her vain attempt to interest that inexorable dowager; 'but my brother Wilmot seems to have a great deal to say to her, and if I have a passion for one thing above another, it is for family portraits, especially where the family is ancient and distinguished like yours.'

'O, very well, you can come, of course. I'll show you the old fogies; my grandfathers and great-grandfathers, and all their brotherhood and sister-hood.'

'Miss Disney will accompany us, of course,' said Mrs. Chevenix, smiling graciously at Hilda, who sat opposite to her, very fair to look upon in her waxwork serenity.

'O, Hilda knows the pictures by heart. She'd rather sit by the fire and spin; or go on with those everlasting accounts she is always scribbling for my mother.'

'I will come if you like, Mrs. Chevenix,' replied Hilda, ignoring her cousin's remark.

The party of exploration, therefore, consisted of

three damsels, Mrs. Chevenix and Lord Paulyn ; a
party large enough to admit of being divided—a result
which aunt Chevenix had laboured to achieve.   Lord
Paulyn straggled off at once with Elizabeth through
the long suite of upper chambers, with deep oaken
seats in all the windows—Hampton Court on a small
scale—leaving Hilda to play cicerone for Mrs. Chevenix and Diana, whom her aunt contrived to keep
at her side.   This left the coast clear for the other
two, whose careless laughter rang gaily through the
old empty rooms.   Merciless was the criticism which
those departed Paulyns suffered at the hands of their
graceless descendant and Elizabeth Luttrell.   The
scowling military uncles, the blustering naval uncles,
the smirking grandmothers and aunts, with powdered
ringlets meandering over bare shoulders, or flowing
locks and loose bodice of the Lely period.   Lord
Paulyn entertained his companion with scraps of
family history ; their mesalliances, extravagances,
and other misdeeds, which did not tend to the glori-
fication of that noble race.

But Reginald Paulyn did not devote all his attention to his duties as cicerone.   He had a great deal
to say to Elizabeth about himself and his own affairs ;
and a great many questions to ask about herself, her
likings, dislikings, and so on.

'I'm sure you're fond of horses,' he said; 'a girl with your superior intellect must be fond of horses.' •

'I did not know that taste was a mark of superior intellect; I may have a dormant passion for horse-flesh, certainly, but you see it has never been developed. I can't go into raptures about Toby, that big horse you saw in the wagonette. I used to be very fond of Cupid, a pony that Blanche and I rode when we were children; but unfortunately Cupid grew too small for me, or at least I grew too big for Cupid, and papa gave him away. That is all my experience of horses.'

'Bless my soul!' exclaimed the Viscount, with a distressed air. 'It seems a burning shame that a girl like you should get so little out of life. Why, you ought to have a couple of hunters, and follow the hounds twice a week every season; it would be an introduction to a new existence. And you ought to have a pair of thorough-bred ponies, and a nice little trap to drive them in.'

Elizabeth laughed gaily at this suggestion.

'A clergyman's daughter with her own hunters and pony-carriage would be rather an incongruous person,' she said.

'But you're not going to be a clergyman's daugh-

ter all your life. When you come to London you'll
see things in a very different light.'

'London,' repeated Elizabeth, with a little sigh.
'Yes, I think I should like that kind of life; only the
poor old home will seem ever so much more dismal
afterwards. I sometimes fancy I could bear it better
if there were not quite so many Sundays. The week-
days would go drifting by, and one would hardly know
how long the dreary time was, any more than one
counts the hours when one is asleep. But Sunday
pulls you up sharply with the reflection—"Another
empty week gone; another empty week coming!" A
day of rest, too, after a week of nothingness. What a
mockery!'

'Sunday is a bore, certainly,' said the Viscount.
'People are so dam prejudiced. If it wasn't for
Tattersall's, and the Star-and-Garter—a rather jolly
dinner-place near town, you know—Sunday would be
unbearable. But I wouldn't worry myself about coming back to Hawleigh after you've had a season in
town, if I were you. Sufficient for the day, you
know, as that fellow Shakespeare says. In the first
place, it's a long way ahead; and in the second, you
may never come back at all. Who knows?'

They were sitting on one of the deep old window-
seats, waiting for the two young ladies and Mrs. Che-

venix, that diplomatic person having contrived to ask
Hilda so many questions about the pictures, and to
be so fascinated ever and anon by glimpses of that
flat waste of verdure called the park, as to detain her
party for some time by the way, thus affording Elizabeth and the Viscount ample leisure for their tête-à-
tête. They were sitting side by side in one of the
windows ; Elizabeth with her head resting against
the ponderous shutter, the golden-brown hair melting
into the rich-brown of the polished oak, the heavy
eyelids drooping lazily over the dark-blue eyes, the
whole face in a half listless repose. Very different
would have seemed the same face if Malcolm Forde
had been her companion—radiant with a light and
life whose glory Reginald Paulyn was destined never
to behold.

'You can't tell what's in the future, you see,'
said the Viscount, looking curiously at the tranquil
face opposite him. 'Suppose I were to tell your fortune—eh, Miss Luttrell ?' .

'I should have to cross your palm with a piece of
gold, perhaps, and I'm sure I haven't any.'

'Never mind the gold. Shall I tell you your
fortune ?'

'I have no great faith in your prophetic power.'

'You wouldn't say that if you saw my betting-book.

I have not been out in my calculations three times since the Craven meeting.'

' But that is quite another matter ; you have some solid groundwork for your calculations there ; and here you have none.'

' Haven't I ? Yes, I have ; only you'd be offended if I were to tell you what it is. I must have your hand, please—no, the left,' as she offered him the right with a somewhat reluctant air. ' Yes, in this pretty little pink palm I can read a great deal. First and foremost, that it will be your own fault if ever you go back to Hawleigh parsonage as Miss Luttrell ; secondly, that you can have as many hunters as you like at your disposal next winter ; thirdly, that it will be your own fault if you have not your pony-carriage and outriders for the park in the following spring. That's my prophecy. Of course it will depend in a considerable measure upon yourself whether I prove a true prophet.'

Elizabeth's heart beat a little faster as Lord Paulyn released her hand, with just the faintest detention of those slim fingers in his strong grasp. Was not this the very realisation of her brightest, fondest dream of earthly glory ? Rank and wealth, fashion and pleasure and splendour, seemed, as it were, flung into her lap, like a heap of gathered roses,

without trouble or effort of her own to compass their
winning; prizes in life's lottery that she had only
thought of in a far-off way, as blessings which might
come to her sooner or later, if fortune were kind—
but prizes that she had thought of very much and
very often—to be cast thus at her feet! For, although the Viscount had not in plain words offered
her his hand and fortune, there was a significance in
his tone, an earnestness in his looks, that made his
speech almost a preliminary offer—a sounding of the
ground, before taking a bolder step.

She gave a little silvery laugh, which seemed a
sufficient reply to Lord Paulyn's vaticination.

Even in that moment, with a vision of horses and
carriages, country seats and opera-boxes, shining before her; dazzled with the thought of how grand a
thing it would be actually to win the position she had
talked of winning only in her wildest, most insolent
moods; to prove to Gertrude and Diana, and all the
little world which might have doubted or disparaged
her, that she was indeed a superior creature, marked
out by destiny for a splendid career—even amid such
thoughts as these, there came the image of Malcolm
Forde, a disturbing presence.

'Could I bear my life without him?' she thought;
'could I ever put him quite out of my mind?'

All her **worldly** longings, **her** ignorant yearning for the splendours of this world, seemed hardly strong enough to weigh against that foolish passion for a man who had never professed any warmer regard for **her** than for the most commonplace young woman in **his congregation.**

'**If** he loved me, and asked me to be his wife, should **I be foolish** enough **to marry** him, I wonder?' she thought, while Lord Paulyn's admiring gaze was still rooted to her thoughtful face; '**would** I give **up every pleasure I** have ever dreamed about **for his sake ?'**

The Viscount was happily unconscious of the turn which **his** companion's thoughts had taken. **He** fancied that it was **his own** suggestive remarks which had made her thoughtful.

'**I** fancy I hit her rather hard there,' he said to himself. '**I** don't suppose **it will** ever come to anything, and **I've** made my book so as to hedge the matrimonial question altogether; **but if** ever I do marry, that's the girl I'll have for my wife. Not **a** sixpence to bless herself with, of course—and there are no **end of** young **women in** the market who'd **bring me a hatful of** money—but a man can't have **everything, and a** girl who'd been **brought up in a** Devonshire parsonage wouldn't **be** likely **to have** any extravagant notions calculated to ruin a fellow.'

By which sagacious reflection it will be seen that the Viscount was not without the Paulyn virtue of economy.

Hilda's calm presence appeared anon upon the threshold of the open door, leading the way for the others; and this being the last of the state rooms, the Viscount's opportunities came to an end. He was hardly sorry for this, perhaps, having said already rather more than he wanted to say. 'But that girl is handsome enough to make any fellow lose his head,' he said to himself, by way of excuse for his own imprudence.

Miss Disney surveyed the two with a thoughtful countenance. 'I hope you have been entertained with the pictures, Miss Elizabeth,' she said, with the faintest possible sneer; 'I had no idea that Reginald was so accomplished a critic as to keep you amused all this time.'

'We haven't been looking at the pictures or talking of the pictures half the time,' replied Elizabeth coolly. 'You don't imagine one could interest oneself for an hour with those dingy old portraits. We have been talking of ourselves—always a most delightful subject.'

Miss Disney smiled a wintry smile.

'Then if we have done with the pictures, we may as well go back to my aunt,' she said.

'O, hang it all,' exclaimed Lord Paulyn, looking at his watch, a bulky hunter that had been over more five-barred gates and bullfinches than fall to the lot of many timepieces, 'there's an hour and a half before dinner; we can't shiver in that Siberian drawing-room all that time. Put on your wraps, and come for a walk in the park, and I'll take you round to the stables and show you my hunters.'

Anything seemed preferable, even to aunt Chevenix, to that dreary drawing-room with its handful of fuel; so the ladies clad themselves in shawls and winter jackets, and sallied out with Lord Paulyn to inspect his domain.

There was very little to see in the park—a vast expanse of flat greensward dotted about by some fine old timber; here and there a young plantation of sycamore and poplar—the dowager affected only the cheapest kind of timber—looking pinched and poor in its leaflessness, protected by a rugged post-and-rail fence, with Lady Paulyn's initials branded upon every rail, lest midnight marauders should plunder her fences in their lawless quest for firewood. It was all very sombre and dreary in the early November twilight, and the black moorland above them took a threatening aspect, as of a sullen giant meditating some vengeance against the house of Ashcombe, which had lain a vassal at his feet so long.

'I would rather have the humblest cottage perched up yonder on the summit of that hill,' cried Elizabeth, pointing to the dark edge of the moor, behind which the faint yellow light was fading, 'than this grand house down here; there's something stifling in the atmosphere.'

'You'd find it uncommonly cold up yonder in the winter,' replied the Viscount in his practical way; 'and Ashcombe wouldn't be half a bad place if it was properly kept up, with about six times the establishment my mother keeps. But she has her whims, poor old lady, and I'm bound to give way to them as long as she's mistress here.'

'How good of you!' said Hilda; 'how very good of you, to allow my aunt to deprive herself of luxuries and pleasures in order that you may be the richest man in the county!'

'You needn't indulge your natural propensity for sneering, at my expense, Miss Disney,' replied Lord Paulyn rather savagely. 'It amuses my mother to save money, and I let her do it. Just as I should let her keep a roomful of tame cats if she had a fancy

that way. I don't think your position in the family
is one that gives **you a** right **to** criticise my conduct.'

The fair transparent **face** flushed faintly for **a**
moment, but Miss Disney vouchsafed no answer ;
and Diana Luttrell plunged valorously into the gap
with an eager demand to see the hunters before **it**
grew **quite** dark.

'Very **proper indeed,'** thought Mrs. Chevenix ;
' **that kind of young woman requires** a good deal of
putting **down.   I never like these** dependent cousins
about a young man—especially if they happen to be
good-looking.'

She glanced at Miss Disney, a slim graceful figure
of about middle height, dressed in a shabby black silk
gown, but with a certain elegance that was independent
of dress.   **A fair delicate face,** in whose thoughtful
calm the Chevenix eye could discover very little. **She**
had only a general impression that these quiet young
women are of all others the most dangerous.

They went to the stables to see Lord Paulyn's
horses ; and **Mrs. Chevenix** had to endure rather an
uncomfortable **quarter of an** hour going **in** and out
of loose boxes, **where** satin-coated steeds with fiery
eyes jerked and champed and snorted at her with
malignant intentions, or seemed so to champ and

snort; but she bore it all with a lamb-like meekness:
while Elizabeth patted the velvety noses of these
creatures with her ungloved hand, and stood fearlessly beside them in a manner that went far to con-
firm the Viscount's belief in her vast superiority to
the common order of women. Not that Hilda Disney
showed any fear of the horses. She was as much at
home with them as if they had been so many lap-
dogs, and they seemed to know and love her, a fact
which Mrs. Chevenix marked with a jealous eye.

'Love me, love my dog,' she thought; 'some
people begin by loving the dog.'

It was dark when they left the great gloomy quadrangle where the long row of loose boxes had the air
of so many cells for solitary confinement, and Miss
Disney conducted them to one of the numerous spare
bedrooms to readjust their toilets for the evening, a
bedroom which was spare in every sense of the word;
sparely furnished with an ancient four-poster and
half a dozen grim high-backed chairs, a darksome
mahogany dressing-table, a tall narrow looking-glass
which was a most impartial reflector of the human
countenance, making every one alike hideous; sparely
lighted with a single candle in a massive silver can-
dlestick, engraved with the Paulyn arms. Here Hilda
left them to their own devices. There was no offer

of afternoon tea, and Diana yawned dismally as she cast herself upon one of the high-backed chairs.

'How I wish it was over!' she exclaimed; 'I don't think I ever had such a long day. It's all very well for Lizzie, she has Lord Paulyn to flirt with, and I suppose it's rather nice to flirt with a Viscount. But Miss Disney is really the most un-get-on-able-with girl that it was ever my misfortune to encounter.'

'Miss Disney is a very clever young woman, my dear, for all that,' replied Mrs. Chevenix mysteriously; 'rely upon it, she has her own views about her position here.'

'You mean that she would like to marry her cousin, I suppose,' said Elizabeth.

'I mean that to do that is the sole aim and object of her life,' replied Mrs. Chevenix with conviction, 'but a design in which she will not succeed.'.

'You're so suspicious, auntie,' said Elizabeth carelessly. 'Aren't we to have any more candles? O, dear me, what a dreadful old place this is!—something like those goblin castles one reads of in German legends, where there are a number of huge ancient rooms and only one old steward, and where a traveller begs a night's shelter, and is half frightened to death before morning.'

The dinner, which Elizabeth had looked forward to seeing as a kind of natural curiosity, was of a somewhat shadowy and Barmecide order, like the pale wraith of some decent dinner that had died and been buried a long while ago. There was Julienne, that refuge of the destitute in soups, a thin and vapid decoction, with a faint flavour of pot-herbs and old bones; there was filleted sole à la maître d'hôte, with a good deal more sauce—a compound of the bill-sticker-and-paste-brush order—than sole. There was curry, that rock of refuge for the distressed cook —a curry which might have been veal or rabbit, or the remains of the ancient fowl that had graced the board at luncheon; and there were patties also, of a somewhat flavourless order, patties that were curiously lacking in individuality. The joint is a more serious thing, and the cook, feeling that her art was here unavailing, came to the front boldly with a very small leg of Dartmoor mutton, which gave place anon to a brace of pheasants, the victims of Lord Paulyn's gun. The sweets were various preparations of a gelatinous and farinaceous order, stately in shape and appearance, and faintly flavoured with Marsala, or essential oil of almonds. The dessert consisted of biscuits, and almonds and raisins, a dish of wintry apples, and another of half-ripened oranges, and some fossil preparations of crystallised fruit, which looked liked heir-looms that had been handed down from generation to generation of the Paulyns. This banquet —served with a solemn air, and a strict observance of the proprieties, by the ancient man-of-all-work and a puritanical-looking parlour-maid, who evidently had the ancient under her thumb, and who gibed at him and scolded him ever and anon in the retirement of the sideboard—was a somewhat dreary meal; but Lord Paulyn had Elizabeth on his left hand, and found plenty to talk about with that damsel while the barren courses dragged their slow length along. Mr. Luttrell, to whom a good dinner was the very mainstay of existence, sought in vain to satisfy his appetite with the insignificant morsels of provision that were handed him by the ancient serving-man; nor was he able to console himself for the poverty of the menu by a desperate recourse to the bottle; for the vintages which the ancient doled out to him were of so thin and sour a character, that he was inclined to think the still hock was more nearly related to the dowager's own peculiar brand of cider than that lady would have cared to acknowledge. He ate his dinner, however, or made believe to eat, with a cheerful countenance, heroically concealing the anguish that gnawed him within, and did his best to make himself agreeable to Lady Paulyn, who was a strong-minded old woman, read every line of the *Times* newspaper daily, and was up in all the ins and outs of the money market, being much given to the shifting of her investments, and to cautious little speculations and dabblings on her own account. The Vicar, who had never had a sixpence to invest, found it rather up-hill work to discuss foreign loans, Indian irrigation companies, and American railways with this astute financier, and was glad when the conversation drifted into a political channel, when the dowager proclaimed herself an advanced liberal, with revolutionary notions about the income-tax.

He was hardly sorry when they all left the table together, after a small ration of very indifferent coffee had been served out by the ancient, 'in the nice friendly continental fashion,' as the dowager remarked with a sprightly air, and he found a quiet little dark corner in the drawing-room—dimly illumined with two pair of sallow-complexioned candles, which gave a sickly light, as if just recovered from the jaundice—where he sank into a peaceful and soothing slumber, while Lady Paulyn played fox-and-geese with Mrs. Chevenix, who was enraptured by this small token of favour from the dowager. Lord Paulyn insisted upon playing bézique in a remote corner with Elizabeth,

leaving Diana and Hilda to languish in solitude on
one of the Grecian couches, Diana making feeble
little attempts at conversation, which Miss Disney
would neither encourage nor assist.

Bézique, which neither of the players cared about
playing, afforded a delightful opportunity for flirtation, in a shadowy corner, where the four languishing
candles made darkness visible; and it was an opportunity which Lord Paulyn contrived to make the most
of. Yet he was careful, withal, not to commit himself to anything serious. There was always plenty
of time for that kind of thing, and he had some years
ago made up his mind never to marry, unless marriage should offer itself to him backed by very substantial advantages in the way of worldly wealth.
But this girl, this country parson's daughter, had
attracted and fascinated him as no other woman had
ever done. He had, indeed, from his boyhood cherished an antipathy to feminine society, preferring to
take his ease in a public billiard-room or a stable-
yard, rather than to sacrifice to the graces of life in
a drawing-room or boudoir. He was not in the least
degree like that typical Frenchman of modern French
novels who spends his forenoon in arraying himself
like the lilies of the field, and then sallies forth,
combed and curled and perfumed, to languish in the

boudoir of the young Marquise de la Rochevielle till dinner-time, and after dining elaborately at the Café Riche, repairs to the side-scenes of some easy-going theatre, to worship at the shrine of Mademoiselle Battemain the dancer; thus employing his life from morn till midnight in the cultivation of the tender passion.

Not often did Reginald Paulyn meet with a woman whose society he considered worth having; but there was in Elizabeth's manner something that charmed him almost as much as her beauty. She was so perfectly at her ease with him; showed at times an insolent depreciation of him, which was refreshing by its novelty; received his adulation with such an air of divine right, that he felt a delightful sense of security in her society. She was not trying to captivate him, like almost all the other young women of his acquaintance. Her mind was not filled to the brim with the one fact that he was the best match of the season.

'Do you think your father would let you ride,' he asked, 'if I were to put a couple of horses at your disposal, and a steady-going old groom I've got down here, who'd take no end of care of you?'

'I am quite sure papa would not; and even if he would, I have no time for riding.'

'No time! Why, what can you find to occupy you down here?'

'I have my poor people to visit.'

'What!' exclaimed the Viscount, with a look of mingled disgust and mortification. 'You don't mean to say that you go in for that kind of thing? I thought your eldest sister did it all.'

'I don't see why my sister should have a copyright in good works.'

'No; but, really, I thought it was quite out of your line.'

'Thanks for the compliment. But you see, I am not quite so bad as I seem. I have taken to visiting some of papa's poorer parishioners lately, and I have found the work much pleasanter than I fancied it would be.'

'O, you have taken to it lately,' said Lord Paulyn, with a moody look. 'I suppose it was that tall curate who put it into your head.'

'Yes; it was Mr. Forde who first awakened me to a sense of my duty,' replied Elizabeth fearlessly.

'How long has he been here, that fellow?'

'What fellow?'

'The Curate.'

'Mr. Forde has been with us nearly two years.'

After this the conversation languished a little, while Lord Paulyn meditated upon the possibilities with regard to Miss Luttrell and her father's curate. She had flashed out at him so indignantly just now, as if his disrespectful mention of this man were an offence to herself. He determined to push the question a little closer.

'I daresay he's a very decent fellow,' he said; 'but I could never make much way with men of that kind. They seem a distinct breed somehow, like the zebra. However, I've no doubt he's a well-meaning fellow. I thought he seemed rather sweet upon your eldest sister.'

Elizabeth gave a little scornful laugh.

'Mr. Forde is not sweet upon any one,' she answered; 'he is a priest for ever, after the order of Melchisedec; or after a more severe order, for I believe that matrimony was not forbidden to that ancient priesthood. Mr. Forde sets his face against it.'

'An artful dodge upon his part, perhaps,' said the Viscount doubtfully. 'I daresay he is lying in wait for a wife worth having.'

His keen eyes surveyed Elizabeth's face with a searching gaze, but could not read the mystery of that splendid countenance. He would have gone on

talking about the Curate, but she checked him with
an authoritative air.

'I wouldn't trouble myself to discuss Mr. Forde's
inclinations, if I were you,' she said; 'you have
confessed your inability to sympathise with that
kind of person. He is a noble-minded man, who
has marked out a particular line of life for himself. There is nothing in common between you and
him.'

'Candid,' said the Viscount with a careless laugh,
'but not complimentary. No, I don't suppose *my*
line of life is what you'd call noble-minded; but I
mean to win a Derby before I die; and I mean to win
something else too'—this with the bright red-brown
eyes full upon her face—'if I make up my mind to
go in for it.'

The wagonette was announced at this juncture,
and Mr. Luttrell awoke from refreshing slumbers to
gather his womankind around him and depart from
the halls of Ashcombe, rejoicing in his soul at this
release.

'Thank goodness, that's over!' he exclaimed, as
he settled himself in a corner of the wagonette, half
smothered by his sister's ample draperies and cash-
mere shawl; 'and if ever Lady Paulyn catches me
trusting myself to her hospitality again, she may

give me as miserable a dinner as she gave me to-day.'

'Upon my word, Wilmot, I believe you are the most short-sighted of created beings,' exclaimed Mrs. Chevenix, with a profound sigh.

'It would have required an uncommonly long sight to see anything fit to eat at that dinner,' answered Mr. Luttrell. 'Supper is a meal to which I have a radical objection; but if there's anything edible in the house when we get home to-night, I shall be strongly tempted to submit my digestion to that ordeal.'

'I'm sure I could eat half a barrel of oysters,' exclaimed Diana with a weary air. 'I never went through such a day in my life. It's all very fine for aunt Chevenix and Lizzie to be puffed up with the idea of having made a conquest, but anybody can see that Lord Paulyn is a professed flirt, and that his attentions are as meaningless as they can be.'

'These are questions,' said aunt Chevenix with dignity, 'which time alone can solve. I think we have had an extremely pleasant day, and that Lady Paulyn is a woman of wonderful force of character. Eccentric I admit, and somewhat close in her domestic arrangements—I'm afraid my cap was on one side all the evening, from the inadequacy of light on the toilet-table when I dressed for dinner—but a very remarkable woman.'

'That's a safe thing to say of anybody, aunt,' replied Elizabeth. 'Mrs. Brownrigg, who starved her apprentices to death, was a remarkable woman.'

CHAPTER X.

'Who knows what's fit for us? Had fate
Proposed bliss here should sublimate
My being—had I sign'd the bond—
Still one must lead some life beyond,   .
Have a bliss to die with, dim-descried.'

WHETHER Lord Paulyn's attentions were indeed
meaningless, or whether serious intentions tending
towards matrimony lurked behind them, was a question whose solution Time, the revealer of all secrets,
did not hasten to afford. The Viscount spent about
three weeks in Devonshire, during which period he
contrived to see a good deal of the vicarage people—
calling at least twice a week, upon one pretence or
another, and dragging out each visit to its extremest
length. He was not an intellectual person, and had
contrived to exist since the conclusion of his university career without opening a book, except only such
volumes as could assist him in the supervision of his
stables, or aid his calculations as a speculator on the
turf. His conversation was therefore in no manner

enlivened or adorned by the wit and wisdom of others; but he had a little stock of anecdotes and reminiscences of his career in the fashionable world, and of the 'fellows' he had encountered there, wherewith to entertain his hearers. He had also a yacht, the Pixy, whose performances were a source of interest to him, and which afforded an occasional variety to his stable-talk. In fact, he made himself so agreeable in a general way, during his visits to the Vicarage, that Mrs. Chevenix pronounced him the most entertaining and original young man it had ever been her good fortune to encounter.

Elizabeth was not always at home when he called, but he contrived to spin-out his visit until her return; an endeavour in which he was much assisted by Mrs. Chevenix, who took care to acquaint him with her disapproval of this parish work, and her fear that dear Elizabeth was undermining her health by these pious labours.

'If she were an ordinary girl, I should regard the thing in quite another light,' said aunt Chevenix; 'but Elizabeth is not an ordinary girl.' An opinion in which the Viscount concurred with enthusiasm.

'It's all that Curate's doing,' he said. 'Why don't you use your influence against that fellow, Mrs. Chevenix?'

'O, you're jealous of the Curate, are you?' thought the matron; 'then perhaps we can bring you on a little faster by that means.'

She gave a plaintive sigh, and shook her head doubtfully.

'I regret to say that my influence goes for nothing when Mr. Forde is in question,' she said. 'He has contrived to impress Elizabeth with the idea that he is a kind of saint.'

'You don't think she cares for him?' asked the Viscount eagerly.

'Not in the vulgar worldly sense of the words, dear Lord Paulyn,' said Mrs. Chevenix; 'but she has a sensitive impressionable nature, and he has contrived to exercise an influence which sometimes alarms me. She is a girl who would hardly astonish me if she were to go over to Rome, and immure herself for life in a convent.'

'That would be a pity,' said the Viscount; 'and it would be a greater pity if she were to marry some stick of a curate.'

But he did not commit himself to any stronger expression than this; and he left Devonshire without making Elizabeth Luttrell an offer; — a fact which gave rise to a few sisterly sarcasms on the part of Gertrude and Diana. Blanche was more good-

natured, and was really desirous of having a noble-
man for her brother-in-law.

But before he departed from his native place Lord
Paulyn dined two or three times at the Vicarage,
having hung about late in the afternoon in such a
manner as to invite Mr. Luttrell's hospitality. 'I
don't much wonder that he shirks his mother's dinners,' remarked that short-sighted incumbent; nor
did he see any special cause for self-gratulation when
the Viscount spent his evenings in hanging over the
piano while Elizabeth sang, or in teaching her the
profound theories of écarté.

If the Vicar was slow to perceive anything peculiar in this gentleman's conduct, there were plenty of
more acute observers in Hawleigh who kept a record
of his movements, and told each other over afternoon
tea-cups that Lord Paulyn must be smitten by one
of the vicarage girls.

Before the young man had left the neighbourhood, this rumour had reached the ears of Malcolm
Forde.

He heard this scrap of gossip with a somewhat
bitter smile, remembering the Sunday luncheon at
the Vicarage, and to whom the Viscount's attention
had been exclusively given.

'I am hardly sorry for it,' he said to himself.

'God knows that I have fought against my own folly in loving her so dearly—loving her with no higher hope or thought than a passionate delight in her beauty, a blind worship of herself, a sinful indulgence for her very faults, which have seemed in her so many additional charms; knowing her all the while to be the last of women to help me on in the path that I have chosen for myself, the very woman to hold me backward, to keep me down by the dead weight of her worldliness. I shall have reason to be grateful to Lord Paulyn if he comes between us, and makes a sudden end of my madness.'

Yet, with a curious inconsistency, when the Curate met Elizabeth in one of the cottages, he saluted her with so gloomy a brow and so cold an air that the girl went home miserable, wondering how she had offended him. That he could be jealous was an idea that never entered into her mind, for she had never hoped that he loved her. She went home that afternoon thinking him the coldest and hardest of mankind—a man whose gloomy soul no act of submission could conciliate; went home and avenged herself for that outrage by a desperate flirtation with the Viscount, who happened to eat his farewell dinner at the Vicarage that evening.

Lord Paulyn departed and made no sign: yet it

is certain that he left Hawleigh as deeply in love with
Elizabeth Luttrell as it was in his nature to love any
woman upon this earth. But he was a gentleman of
a somewhat cold and calculating temper, and was
supported and sustained in all the events of life by
an implicit belief in his own merits, and the value of
his position and surroundings. He was not a man
to throw himself away lightly. Elizabeth was a
charming girl, and, in his opinion, the handsomest
woman he had ever seen, and the very fittest to lend
a grace and glory to his life in the eyes of his fellow
men—a wife he might be proud to see pointed out as
his property on racecourses, or on the box-seat of his
drag, as his favourite team drew themselves together
for the start, on a field-day at Hyde-park Corner.
But on the other hand, there was no denying that
such a match would be a very paltry alliance for him
to make, bringing him neither advantageous connec-
tions nor addition to his fortune; and if on sober reflection, at a distance from the object of his passion,
he found that he could live without Elizabeth Luttrell, why he might have reason to congratulate
himself upon his judicious withdrawal from that too
delightful society.

'Mind, I shall expect to see you in town early in
the season,' he said to Elizabeth, when making his

adieux. A speech which he felt committed him to nothing.

'You mustn't forget your promise to show us the university boat-race,' said Mrs. Chevenix with her vivacious air.

She felt not a little disappointed that nothing more decisive had come of the young man's admiration; that he should be able thus to tear himself away unfettered and uncompromised. She had fondly hoped that he would linger on at Ashcombe till in some impassioned moment he should cast his fortunes at the feet of his enchantress. It was somewhat bitter therefore to see him depart in this cool manner, with only vague anticipations of possible meetings during the London season. Mrs. Chevenix was well aware of a fact which the Viscount pretended to ignore, namely, that her set was not his set, and that it was only by means of happy accidents or diplomatic struggles that she and her niece could hope to meet him in society.

' But he will call, no doubt,' she said to herself, having taken especial care to furnish him with her address.

Elizabeth gave a great sigh of relief as the vicarage door closed for the last time upon her admirer. She had been gratified by his admiration, she had listened to him with an air of interest, had brightened and sparkled as she talked to him; but it was dull work at the best. There was no real sympathy, and it was an unspeakable relief to know that he was gone.

'Thank heaven that's over!' she exclaimed; 'and now I can live my own life again.'

After the Viscount's departure Mrs. Chevenix began to find life at Hawleigh a burden too heavy for her to bear. The ceremonial call which she and her two nieces had made at Ashcombe about a week after the dinner there, had resulted in no new invitation, nor in any farther visit from Lady Paulyn. Intimacy with the inexorable dowager, which aunt Chevenix had done her utmost to achieve, was evidently an impossibility. So about a week before Christmas Mrs. Chevenix and her confidential maid left the Vicarage, to the heartfelt satisfaction of Mr. Luttrell's household, and not a little to the relief of that hospitable gentleman himself.

December was nearly over. A long dreary month it had seemed to Elizabeth; and since that Sunday luncheon at which Lord Paulyn had assisted, Malcolm Forde had paid no visit to the Vicarage. Elizabeth had seen him two or three times in the course of her district-visiting, and on each occasion he had seemed to her colder and sterner of manner than on the last.

Gertrude was the only member of the family who made any remark upon this falling away of Mr. Forde's. The Vicar knew that he worked harder than any other labourer who had ever come into that vineyard, and was not surprised that he should lack leisure for morning calls; nor had he ever been a frequent visitor at the Vicarage. But Gertrude remarked with an injured air that of late he had ceased from calling altogether.

'I've no doubt he heard that Lord Paulyn was always here,' she observed; 'and of course that kind of society would not be likely to suit him.'

'I can't see that papa's curates have any right to select our society for us,' exclaimed Blanche, firing up at this. 'Lord Paulyn was no particular favourite of mine, for he used to take about as much notice of me as if I were a chair or a table; and Mr. Forde is always nice; but still I can't see that he has any right to object to our visitors.'

'No one spoke of such a right, Blanche,' answered her eldest sister; 'but Mr. Forde is free to select his own society, and it is only natural that he should avoid a person of Lord Paulyn's calibre.'

Elizabeth felt this defection keenly. It was not

as if she had neglected her duties, or fallen away
from the right path in any palpable manner. She
had gone on with her work unflinchingly, even when,
depressed by *his* coldness, her spirits had flagged and
the work had grown wearisome. She had been constant in her attendance at the early services on dismal winter mornings, when the outer world looked
bleak and uninviting. She had struggled to be good,
according to her lights, perceiving no sinfulness in
that flirtation with Lord Paulyn, which had helped
to fill her empty life.

She missed the excitement of these flirtations
when Lord Paulyn was gone. It was all very well to
declare that he had bored her, and to express herself
relieved by his departure; but she missed that agreeable ministration to her vanity. It had been pleasant
to know, when she made her simple toilet for the
home dinner, that every fresh knot of ribbon in her
hair made her lovelier in the eyes of a man whose
admiration the world counted worth winning—pleasant to discover that fascinations which had no power
to touch the cold heart of Malcolm Forde possessed
an overwhelming influence for the master of Ashcombe. Yet the end of her flirtation with the Viscount
was hardly less humiliating to her than the coldness
of the Curate. He loved and he rode away. She

began to think that she had no real power over the hearts of men ; that she could only startle and bewitch them by her beauty; hold them for but the briefest space in her thrall.

If the Viscount's admiration had gone a step farther, and he had made her an offer, what would have been her reply ? That was a question which she had asked herself many times of late, and for which she could find no satisfactory answer. The prospect was almost too dazzling for her to contemplate with a steady gaze. Had not a brilliant marriage been the dream of her girlhood ? a vision first evoked by some prophetic utterances of aunt Chevenix, when Elizabeth was only a tall slip of a girl in a pinafore practising major and minor scales on a battered old piano in the school-room. She had dreamed of horses and carriages, and opera-boxes and country-seats, from the hour when she first learned the value of her growing loveliness at the feet of that worldly teacher. All that was basest in her nature, her ignorant yearning for splendour and pleasure, her belief in her divine right to be prosperous and happy, had been fostered, half unconsciously perhaps, by aunt Chevenix. Mrs. Luttrell was the weakest and simplest of women, and had always referred to her sister-in-law as the very oracle of social existence, and had fondly believed in that lady as a leader of London fashion to her dying day. There had been no home influence in the vicarage household to counteract the Chevenix influence, and although Elizabeth took a pride in defying her aunt upon occasions, she was not the less her faithful disciple.

Could she have refused such an offer from Lord Paulyn? Could she of her own free will have put aside at once and for ever—since two such chances would hardly come in her obscure life—all the delights and triumphs of this world, all the pleasures she had dreamed of? It hardly seemed possible that she could have been so heroic as to say no. It was very certain, on the other hand, that she did not care for Reginald Paulyn, that his handsome face had no charm for her, that the lingering clasp of his strong hand sent no thrill to her heart, that his society after the first half-hour became a bore to her. It was quite as certain that there was another man whose coldest look quickened the beating of her heart, whose lightest touch had a magical influence; for whose sake poverty would seem no hardship, obscurity no affliction; by whose side she could have felt herself strong enough to make life's pilgrimage over ever so thorny a road.

'I could hardly have been so demented as to refuse him,' she thought, remembering that this one man for whom she could have so cheerfully sacrificed all her visions of earthly glory had no desire to profit by her self-abnegation.

Christmas was close at hand, and the Luttrell girls were busy from morning till evening with the decoration of the two churches; but Elizabeth performed her share of this labour with a somewhat listless air, and did a good deal more looking-on than Gertrude or Diana approved. She was beginning to be very tired of her work, tired even of her poor people, despite their affection for her. It seemed altogether such a dreary business, uncheered by Mr. Forde's counsel or approbation; not that he would have withheld his counsel, had she taken the trouble to ask for it; but she could not bring herself to do that. She remembered that October day in the vicarage garden when they had walked together over the fallen leaves, while autumn winds moaned dismally, and autumn clouds obscured the sun—that day when they had seemed so near to each other, and when the dull gray world had been lighted with that light that never was on sea or shore—the light of a great joy. What would she not have done for his sake, if he had only taken the trouble to order her. If he had been a Redemptorist father, and had pre-

sented her with a cat-o'-nine-tails wherewith to go
and scourge herself, she would have taken the whip
from him with a smile, and departed cheerfully to do
his bidding. But he asked no more from her than
from any other member of that little band of ladies
who helped him in the care of his poor, and he distinguished her from that little band only by his
peculiar coldness.

She flung down her garland of ivy and holly with
an impatient air, in the midst of a little cluster of
ladies working busily in the vestry of St. Clement's,
the decorations whereof were but half completed.

'I shall do no more,' she said; 'my fingers ache
and smart horribly. I am tired of the whole business; tired of parish work altogether.'

Miss Melvin looked up at her friend wonderingly,
with her meek blue eyes.

'Why, Lizzie, I'm surprised to hear you say that,'
she exclaimed. 'Mr. Forde says you are the best of
all his district-visitors, because you are sympathetic,
and the poor people understand you.'

'I feel very much honoured by his praise,' said
Elizabeth, with a scornful little laugh; 'but as he
has never taken the trouble to give me the slightest
encouragement of late, I begin to find the work a
little disheartening.'

'Elizabeth has an insatiable appetite for praise,' remarked Gertrude ; 'and I daresay she has been not a little spoiled by Lord Paulyn's absurd flatteries.'

'You have been rather fortunate in escaping that kind of contamination, Gerty,' replied Elizabeth, whose temper was by no means at its best on this particular Christmas-eve ; 'but I assure you it is rather nice to have a viscount for one's slave.'

'Even when his bondage sits so lightly that he is able to shake it off at any moment,' said Gertrude. To which Elizabeth would have no doubt replied, but for the sound of a firm tread upon the stone threshold, and the sudden opening of the door, which had been left ajar by the busy workers.

It was Mr. Forde on his round of inspection. Elizabeth wondered whether he had overheard that shallow unladylike talk about Lord Paulyn. She picked up her unfinished garland, and set to work again hurriedly, glad of any excuse for hiding her face from his cold gaze.

He did not stop long in the vestry, only long enough for a general good-morning, and a few questions about the decorations; nor did he address one word to Elizabeth Luttrell. Her face was still bent over her work, and the wounded fingers were moving busily, when she heard the door shut behind him,

and his departing footstep on the pavement of the
church.

He had come to the vestry-door just in time to
hear Elizabeth's flippant speech about Lord Paulyn ;
a speech which to his mind seemed to reveal the utter shallowness and worthlessness of the woman he
had suffered himself to love.

'And yet she has been able to cheat me into a
belief in the latent nobility of her nature ; she has
been able to bewilder my reason as she has bewitched
my heart,' he said to himself, as he walked slowly
down the quiet aisle, and out into the bleak churchyard ; 'as she has distracted me from better thoughts
and higher hopes, and has been an evil influence in
my life from the first fatal hour in which I let her
creep into my heart.'

Even the Vicar's friendly invitation for Christmas-day was rejected by Mr. Forde.   He would have
been very happy to join that agreeable circle, he wrote,
but it was a pleasure which he felt it safer to deny
himself.   The services on that day were numerous ;
there were sick people he had promised to see in the
course of the day, and he should hardly have time for
anything else, and so on.

He spent his day between the two churches and
those sick-rooms, and his night in solitary reading

and meditation; trying to lift his soul to that higher level whither it had been wont to soar before an earthly passion clogged its wings.

That he would, so far as it was possible to him in his position as Mr. Luttrell's curate, renounce and abjure the society of Mr. Luttrell's daughter, was a resolution that he had arrived at very promptly on hearing the town-talk about Lord Paulyn's frequent visits at the Vicarage.

'I will not trust myself near her,' he said to himself. 'She has deceived me in the past, and would deceive me again in the future. I have no power to resist her witchery, except by separating myself from her for ever.'

He was just strong enough to do this; he had just sufficient force of will to avoid the siren. Knowing the houses in which she was most likely to be found, her customary hours, the way she took in her walks, knowing almost every detail of her daily life, and how easy it would be for him to meet her, not once did he swerve from the rigid line which he had marked out for his conduct: he saw the familiar figure in the distance sometimes, and never quickened his step to overtake it. He heard that she was expected in a cottage where he was visiting, and hurried his departure straightway rather than run the hazard of meeting her. But it is hardly by these means that a man learns to forget the woman he loves. It is a kind of schooling that is apt to end another way. Perhaps no man ever yet forgot by trying to forget: but he is on the highway to forgetfulness when he tries to remember.

A poison had entered into Malcolm Forde's life. That sacred calling which demands the service of a heart uncorrupted by earthly passion began to weigh upon him like a bondage. It was not that he was in any manner weary of his office, but rather that he began to feel himself unfitted for it. A deadly sense of monotony crept into his mind. He began to doubt his powers of usefulness; to fancy that his career at Hawleigh was like the round of a horse in a mill, grinding on for ever, and tending towards no higher result than that common daily bread. The natural result of these languors—these painful doubts of his own worthiness—was to turn his thoughts in that direction whither they had turned not unfrequently in the days when he had been better contented with his lot. He began to think more seriously than ever upon that missionary life which comes nearer to the apostolic form of service than the smooth pastures of the church at home. He collected all the information he could obtain upon this subject; wrote to men who had the work at heart, and who knew where a worker of his stamp was most wanted.

'I have a vigorous constitution,' he wrote to one of his correspondents, 'and have hardly ever known a day's illness. I am therefore not afraid of climate; and if I *do* finally determine to go, I should wish to go where such labour as I can give would be of real value; where a weaker man might be unfit to face the difficulties and dangers which I feel myself qualified to cope with and overcome. Do not think that I am boasting of my strength; I only wish to remind you that my former profession has in some measure inured me to peril and hardship, and that I should be glad to be able to employ some of that military spirit still inherent in my composition in the nobler service to which it is now my privilege to belong. I want to feel myself a soldier and servant of Christ's church militant here on earth, in every sense of the word; and I do not in my present mood find the work of a rural parish adequate for the satisfaction of this desire.'

CHAPTER XI

' 'Tis the pest
Of love, that fairest joys give most unrest ;
That things of delicate and tenderest worth
Are swallow'd all, and made a seared dearth,
By one consuming flame : it doth immerse
And suffocate true blessings in a curse.
Half happy, by comparison of bliss,
Is miserable.'

THAT Christmas at Hawleigh was not a peculiarly festive season. Mr. Luttrell being happily rid of his sister was indisposed for farther society, preferring to bask in the genial glow of his hearth untrammelled by the duties of hospitality. So the Luttrell girls sat round the fire on Christmas evening in a dismal circle, while their father, silent and motionless as the sculptured figure of some household god, slumbered peacefully in his easy-chair behind the banner screen that had shaded the fair features of aunt Chevenix.

'I really do wish that boy-baby had lived,' exclaimed Blanche after a long silence, alluding to an infant scion of the house of Luttrell which had perished untimely. 'Of course, I know he'd have been a nuisance to us all—brothers always are—but still he'd have been something. He must have imparted a little variety to the tenor of our miserable lives. Papa would have been obliged to send him to Oxford or Cambridge, where he would have got into debt for shirt-studs and meerschaum pipes and things, no doubt; but he would have brought home nice young men, perhaps, in the long vacation, and that would be some amusement. He might have touted for papa in a gentlemanly way, and brought home young men to be coached.'

'Blanche,' exclaimed Gertrude, 'you positively grow more revoltingly vulgar in your ideas every day.'

'Let the poor child talk,' cried Diana, with a stifled yawn. 'I wonder she has spirit enough left to be vulgar. Any invertebrate creature can be ladylike, but vulgarity requires a certain amount of animal spirits; and I am sure such a miserable Christmas as this is a damper for any one's vivacity.'

Elizabeth said nothing. She sat on a low seat opposite the fire, motionless as her slumbering father, but with her great dark eyes wide open, gazing dreamily at the smouldering yule log which dropped its white ashes slowly and silently into a deep chasm of dull red coal. She had sat thus for the last half-hour thinking her own thoughts, and taking no part in her sisters' desultory snatches of talk.

' " She sat like Patience on a monument, smiling at grief," ' exclaimed Diana presently, exasperated by this silence, ' Upon my word, Lizzie, you are not the best of company for a winter's night by the fire.'

' I do not pretend to be good company,' replied Elizabeth coolly.

' How different it would be if Lord Paulyn were here !' said Diana, whose temper had been somewhat soured by the dreariness of that long evening; ' then you would be all smiles and bewitchment.'

' I should do my best to entertain a visitor, of course. I do not consider myself bound to entertain you.'

' Poor Lizzie,' murmured Diana, with an insolent air of compassion. ' We ought not to be hard upon you. It is rather a trial for any girl to have a coronet dangled before her eyes in that tantalising manner, and nothing to come of her conquest after all !'

' Do you mean to say that I ever angled for Lord Paulyn,' cried Elizabeth, with a sudden flash of scornful anger, ' or that I could not have him if I chose ?'

' I mean to say,' replied Diana, in a provokingly deliberate manner, ' that you and aunt Chevenix tried your very hardest to catch him, and did not succeed. Perhaps you look forward to seeing him in London, and subjugating him there; but I fancy that if a woman cannot bring an admirer to her feet in the first flush of her conquest, she is hardly likely to bring him there later. He has time for reflection and distraction, you see; and a man who has sufficient prudence to keep himself uncommitted as cleverly as Lord Paulyn did, would be the very man to cure himself of a foolish infatuation. I don't mean to say anything offensive, but of course a marriage with one of us would be a very disadvantageous alliance for a man in his position.'

'You are extremely wise, my dear Di, and have acquired your wisdom in the bitter school of experience. But I doubt if you are quite infallible; and to show you that I am ready to back my opinion, as Lord Paulyn says, I will bet you poor dear mamma's pearl necklace, my only valuable possession, that if he and I live so long, I will be Lady Paulyn before next Christmas-day.'

A foolish wager to make, perhaps, when her heart was given utterly to another man; but these little sisterly skirmishes always brought out the worst points in Elizabeth's character. She had been thinking too, as she watched the softly-dropping ashes, of all the grandeurs and pleasures with which she might have surrounded herself at such a season as this, were she the wife of Viscount Paulyn; thinking of that dismal old house at Ashcombe, and the transformation that she might effect there; the spacious rooms glowing with warm light, filled with pleasant people, new furniture, splendid draperies, life and colour throughout that mansion, where now reigned a death-like gloom and grayness, as if the dust of many generations had settled and become fixed there, covering all things with one sombre hue. These visions were strangely sweet to her shallow soul: and mingled with the thoughts of those possible triumphs there was always the thought of Malcolm Forde, and the impression that such a marriage would make upon him.

'He would see that at least some one can care for me,' she said to herself; 'that if I am not good enough for him, I may be good enough for his superior in rank and fortune.'

And then came a vision of that tall figure and grave face among the witnesses of her wedding. He would take his subordinate part in the service, no doubt; 'by the Vicar of Hawleigh, father of the bride, assisted by the Reverend Malcolm Forde.'

'He would not care,' she thought, 'he would not even be angry with me. But he would preach me a sermon about my increased means of usefulness; he would expect me to become a sister of mercy on a wider scale.'

After that joyless Christmas-time life seemed to Elizabeth Luttrell to become almost intolerable by reason of its dreariness. She gave up her spasmodic attempts at active usefulness altogether. She had emptied her purse for her poor; wearied herself in going to and fro between the Vicarage and their hovels; steeped herself to the lips in their difficulties and sorrows, and to some of them at least had contrived to render herself very dear; and having done this, she all at once abandoned them, stayed at home and brooded upon her vexations, sat for long hours at her piano, playing wild passionate music, which seemed like a stormy voice answering her stormy heart.

'Let him come to me and remonstrate with me again,' she said to herself, looking up with haggard eyes at the drawing-room door, as if she expected to see that tall figure appear at her invocation. 'Let him come to reprove me, and I will tell him that I am tired of working without any earthly reward; that I have neither faith nor patience to labour for

a recompense that I am only to win, perhaps half a
century hence, in heaven. And who knows if I
should see *his* face there, or hear *his* voice praising
me ?'

But the days went by, and Mr. Forde took no
heed of this second defection.

One thing only gave colour to Elizabeth's life in
this hopeless time, and that was the daily service in
the big empty church of St. Clement's, at which she
saw the cold grave face that had usurped so fatal a
power over her soul. Once in every day she must
needs see him ; once in every day she must needs
hear his voice ; and it was to see and hear him that
she rose early on those cheerless winter mornings
and shared the devotions of a few feeble old women
in poke bonnets, and a sprinkling of maiden ladies
with frost-pinched noses showing rosy-tipped beneath
their veils. It was not a pure worship which was
wafted heavenward with Elizabeth's orisons ; rather,
no worship at all, but an impious adoration of the
creature instead of the Creator ; in every word in
the familiar prayers, every sentence in the morning
lessons, she heard the voice of the man she loved,
and nothing more. *His* voice with its slow solemn
depths of music ; *his* face with its earnest eyes for
ever overlooking her. These were the sole elements

of that daily service. She went to church to see and to hear Malcolm Forde, and knew in her heart of hearts that it was for this alone she went; and in some remorseful moments wondered that Heaven's swift vengeance did not descend upon so impious a creature.

'How could I bear my life if I were married to another man and it were a deadly sin to think of him?' she asked herself wonderingly; and then argued with herself that in an utterly new life, a life filled to overflowing with the pleasures that had never yet been within her reach, pleasures that would have all the freshness and delight of novelty, she must surely find it an easy matter to shut Malcolm Forde's image out of her heart.

'In what is he different from all other men, that I should go on lamenting him for ever?' she thought. 'If I lived in the world, I should meet his superiors every day of my life. But living out of the world— seeing only such people as Frederick Melvin and his fellow creatures—it is hardly wonderful that I think him a demi-god.'

And then, in the next moment, with a passionate scorn of her own arguments, she would exclaim:

'But he is above all other men! There is no one like him in that great world I am so ignorant of.

There is no one else whose coldest word could seem sweeter than the praise of other men. There is no one else whose very shadow across my path could be more to me than the love of all the world besides.'

In this blank pause of her life, when all the machinery of her existence, which had for a long time been gradually growing abominable to her by reason of its monotony, seemed all at once to become too hateful for endurance; like a long dusty road, which for a certain distance the pilgrim treads with a kind of hopefulness, until, grown footsore and weary long ere the end of his journey, that long white road under the broiling sun, those changeless hedges, that pitiless burning sky, become an affliction hardly to be borne;—in this sudden failure of happiness and hope it was not unnatural that Elizabeth's eyes should turn with some kind of longing to the dazzling prospect perpetually exhibited to them by aunt Chevenix.

'Remember my dearest Lizzie,' wrote that lady, whose longest epistles were always addressed to Elizabeth—'remember that you have a great future before you, and pray do not suffer yourself to be depressed by any remarks which *envy* or *malice* may dictate to those who *feel themselves* your inferiors in accomplishments and *personal appearance*. Your *fate* is in your own hands, my dearest girl, and it is you alone who can hinder, by a *foolish preference*, of which I cannot think with *common patience*, the very high advancement which I *feel assured* Fortune holds in reserve for you. But I venture to believe that your *absurd admiration* of Mr. F— is a thing of the past. Think, my love, of the delight you would feel in being mistress of a *brilliant establishment*—in finding yourself the centre of an *aristocratic* and *fashionable* circle, invited to *state balls* and *royal garden-parties*—and then contrast this picture with the vision of some obscure parsonage, its Sunday-school, its old women in black bonnets—that species of black bonnet which I imagine must be a natural product of the soil in agricultural districts, so inevitable is its appearance, and I can hardly believe there are people still living who would voluntarily *make* a thing of that shape. Look upon this picture, my dearest girl, and then on that,—as Pope, or some other old-fashioned writer, has observed,—and let reason be your guide. Easter, I am pleased to see, falls early this year, by which means we shall have done with Lent before the fine weather begins. I shall expect you as soon after Easter Sunday as your papa can manage to bring you.'

To this visit she looked forward as a release from

that life which had of late become worse than bondage; but even in this looking forward there was an
element of despair. She might have balls and garden-
parties, and pleasures without number; she might
wear fine dresses, and sun her beauty in the light
of admiring eyes; but she would see Malcolm Forde
no more. Would it not be happier for her to be thus
divided than to see him day by day, and every day
become more assured of his indifference? Yes, she
told herself. And in that whirlpool of London life
was it likely she would be for ever haunted by his
image?

'It is this Mariana-in-the-moated-grange kind
of life that is killing me,' she said to herself, as she
sat by her turret window, preferring her fireless bedroom to the society of her sisters, watching the winter rain fall slowly in the drenched garden, and the
dripping sun-dial by which she had stood so often
talking to Malcolm Forde in the summer that was
gone. It was arranged that Mr. Luttrell and his
third daughter should go to London on the 30th of
March, the Vicar treating himself to a week's holiday
in town, after the fatigue of the Easter services; a
burden which was chiefly borne by the broad shoulders
of Malcolm Forde. Towards the end of February,
therefore, Elizabeth was able to occupy herself with

the pleasing task of preparing for the visit; a business which involved a good deal of dressmaking, and a greater outlay than the Vicar approved. He grumbled and endured, however, as he had grumbled and endured when Gertrude and Diana spread their young pinions for their brief flight into those fashionable skies.

'It seems a nonsensical waste of money,' he said, with a doleful sigh, as he wrote a final clearing-up check for the Hawleigh dressmaker, 'and I don't suppose that your visit will result in anything more than your sisters' visits. But Maria would lead me a life if I refused to let you go.'

'I beg your pardon, papa,' exclaimed Gertrude. 'Pray do not make any comparison between Elizabeth and *us*. She belongs to quite a different order of beings, and is sure to make a brilliant match. It is not to be supposed that the world can overlook *her* merits.'

'I don't know about that,' said the Vicar, with a rueful glance at the figures on his check; 'but this seems a large amount to pay for dressmaking. I think girls in your position—the daughters of a professional man—ought to make your own gowns.'

'The bill isn't all for dressmaking, papa; Miss March has found the material,' said Elizabeth, waiving the question of what a girl in her position ought or ought not to do. 'The trimmings are rather expensive, perhaps; but dresses are so much trimmed nowadays.'

'Yes, that's what I hear on every side, when I complain of my bills,' replied the Vicar. 'Butcher's meat is so much dearer nowadays, says the cook; fodder has risen since last month, says the groom; Russia is consuming our coals, and prices are mounting daily, says the coal-merchant. But unhappily my income is not so elastic—that is a fixed quantity; and I fear the time is at hand when to make that square with our necessities will be something like attempting to square the circle.'

The Luttrell girls were accustomed to mild wailings of this kind when the paternal check-book had to be produced, and checks were signed as reluctantly as if they had been death-warrants waiting for the sign-manual of a tender-hearted king; so they were not deeply impressed by this threat of future destitution. They gave their minds very cheerfully to the preparation of their summer clothing; envied Elizabeth those extra garments provided for her approaching visit; quarrelled and made friends again after the manner of sisters whose affection is tempered by certain individual failings.

Frivolous as the distraction might be, this choosing of colours and materials, and trying-on of new apparel, served to brighten the bleak days of a blusterous March with a feeble light. Elizabeth thought just a little less of her hopeless wasted love, while Miss March's head apprentice was coming to the Vicarage every day with patterns of gimps and fringes and laces and ruchings, for the selection whereof all the sisters had to be convened like a synod. Even Gertrude and Diana were not altogether ill-natured, and gave themselves up to these deliberations with a friendly air; while Blanche flung herself into the subject with youthful ardour, and wound up her approval of every article by the declaration that she would have one like it when she went to aunt Chevenix for *her* London season.

'Or perhaps you'll be married, and have a town-house, Lizzie, and I shall come to you; which would be much nicer than being under auntie's thumb. And of course you'd enjoy bringing out a younger sister. Viscountess Paulyn, on her marriage, by Lucretia Viscountess Paulyn; Miss Blanche Luttrell, by her sister, Viscountess Paulyn. Wouldn't that look well in the local papers?'

END OF VOL. I.

www.ingramcontent.com/pod-product-compliance
Lightning Source LLC
Chambersburg PA
CBHW030623030726
47497CB00006B/1617